ALPHA DRAGON'S JACKAL

The Dragonfate Games Book 3

HAWKE OAKLEY

Hawke's Newsletter

You'll receive an exclusive bonus scene for this book by signing up for my newsletter! You will also be the first to know about new releases, sales, and illustrated art of my boys.

Sign Up Here

or go to www.hawkeoakley.com

HAWKE OAKLEY

ONE

Muzo

THE LAST THING you want to see when you get home from vacation is an eviction notice.

The second season of the Dragonfate Games was over. My blood still buzzed with excitement. I had a blast as usual, but it was nice to be home.

Or so I thought.

After hauling my luggage all the way up the stairs—the apartment elevator was broken again—I paused at the door to my unit. I blinked, clutching my key in hand as I stared at the paper taped up in front of me.

"To Muzo Zavala," I read out loud. "We are terminating your tenancy from Unit 409. Our reason for evicting you is..." I squinted at the next words. "Unlawful dog ownership? Huh?"

What the hell did that mean? I didn't even own a dog.

Frowning in confusion, I looked around the hallway. I wondered if management meant to put the notice on somebody else's door, but the paper had my unit number printed on it, and it was addressed to me. What was going on?

I was exhausted from the flight home, so I figured I'd

deal with it the next day. I plugged the key into the hole... and found that it no longer fit.

"What the heck?" I mumbled.

I twisted and wriggled the key, turning it like I'd done a thousand times, but my attempts were only met with unyielding friction. A sinking feeling washed over me. Management must've changed the lock before I arrived.

"Oh," I said.

I stood there with my now-useless key in one hand and my luggage in the other, not knowing what to do. I expected to come home from the airport and go straight to bed, but now I couldn't do that.

I checked the time on my phone. The management office was still open. Speaking to them was my best option, since there was obviously some kind of mistake. Taking the notice with me, I descended the stairs to the main floor and poked my head into the office's frosted glass door.

"Hello?" I called.

The superintendent, George, glowered at me from behind the counter. He was a middle-aged man with a scary expression. I recognized him since I came here every month to pay rent, but he didn't seem to know me. He had so many tenants that it was probably hard to remember them all. I didn't hold it against him.

I smiled and waved. George's brow furrowed deeper.

"What?" he barked.

I took that as an invitation to enter the room. "Um, hi! I just got home from vacation and I found this notice on my door," I said, pulling out the paper. "I was wondering if it was, er, misplaced?"

George's scowl was a permanent fixture on his face. "Why would it be?"

"Oh, because I don't have a dog," I said cheerfully. That should've cleared up the confusion.

But George's expression didn't budge. "It states very clearly in the contract that pets are not allowed in the building," he ground out. "That includes dogs."

Maybe he didn't hear me properly. He was older, so he could have an auditory processing issue.

"Um, actually, I don't have one. A dog, I mean. Or any pets. I don't even have a house plant," I added with a chuckle.

George exhaled a long, disapproving breath through his nostrils. He broke away from my gaze and shuffled through papers. "That's not what I've been told."

"What?"

"I've had several complaints about a dog in your unit," George grumbled. "Don't bother denying it. A lot of *people* came forward about it."

There was something odd about the way he said 'people.'

"People? Who?" I asked, wondering if it was one of my neighbors.

George narrowed his eyes. "When I say people, I mean *humans*."

He shoved a piece of paper across the counter towards me. I recognized it as the tenancy contract I signed when I first moved in. There was a specific line highlighted—the section about species. It asked if I was human or shifter, and if the latter, to specify what animal. I'd written everything down, because why not? I was proud of who I was, and I thought it was great to have many kinds of people living together.

I blinked down at the paper, then back at George. He met my questioning expression with a flat-out glare.

That was weird. Nobody had ever been so blatantly shifter-phobic to my face before.

"Huh," I said, scratching my head. "It's kinda strange

that they heard a dog in my apartment while I was on vacation, though. Since I wasn't home and all."

George's grouchy expression made it clear he didn't care. "Since you can afford a vacation, you can afford to live somewhere else."

"Er, well, actually, someone else paid for the—"

He interrupted me. "*And* you can afford to find another place to stay tonight. Your belongings are already outside." He jabbed a finger at the counter. "Your key."

There was no room for argument. I deflated as I placed the key in front of him. He snatched it, then proceeded to ignore me. That was worse than glaring.

"Well, see you," I said as I turned to leave. He didn't respond as the door shut behind me. "Or not."

THE DEEP BLUE evening sky greeted me as I walked out into the apartment parking lot. George was right about my belongings—they were shoved haphazardly into cardboard boxes on the curb. Man, it was a good thing I didn't own too much stuff. I was able to cram most of it in my bag or luggage. I left big items like my old couch behind, hoping somebody else could benefit from it.

Once that was done, I had no clue what to do. I sat down on the curb and tilted my head back. A few bright dots sparkled overhead, but the city sky paled in comparison to the sea of stars that lit up the sky on Chromatimaeus Island.

I couldn't help but smile thinking about it. The beauty of that place was unforgettable. I felt so lucky to visit there not once but twice—and to even be invited for a third time. If I closed my eyes, I could still smell the salty ocean breeze, and feel the warm grains of sand between my paw pads...

I shook off a shiver. The memory was so intense, I almost felt a shift coming on, but transforming into my jackal form in front of my shifter-phobic apartment building probably wasn't a great idea.

Well, ex-apartment building now. Did that make me officially homeless?

I stood up and brushed myself off. There was no point in dwelling on it. I checked my phone, which still had juice.

"Better figure out a place to charge this," I said out loud. Maybe at my workplace? I could store my stuff in my locker, too.

Just as I got up, my phone buzzed. I smiled when I saw Poppy's name on the screen.

"Yo, Pops!" I greeted.

"Hi, Muzo," Poppy said gently. Back when we first met, he stammered when greeting me, but he'd gained a lot more confidence since then.

"What's up?" I asked.

I heard a rustling sound on the other end, followed by the *pop* of a food container lid. "Um, I baked a bunch of cookies tonight. Double chocolate."

I gasped. He knew they were my favorite. That was one of the perks of being a shifter. Chocolate made my canine side sick, but my human form could eat as much as my heart desired.

"I haven't left the house all day," Poppy mentioned. "So I thought I could bring them over to you. If you want?"

Of course I wanted. It was sweet that he always asked anyway. I sucked in a breath, eagerly about to tell him to come on over, but then I remembered the fact that I didn't actually live here. Or anywhere.

"Uh," I said.

My brain farted. It was rare that I was at a loss for words. What could I say to him? Not the truth. He lived in a state of constant anxiety—telling him I was homeless might give him a panic attack.

"I... I'm actually out right now," I finished.

"Oh," Poppy murmured. He went quiet for a while, like he didn't know what to say. I couldn't blame him—I'd never, ever refused one of Poppy's cookie runs before. "Um..."

"Hey, why don't you hang onto those cookies, Poppy?" I suggested. "Swing by the BurgerMart tomorrow at eight. I'll be starving after my shift."

That seemed like a good compromise. This way I'd see my friend and get my cookies, he wouldn't know I'd lost my apartment, and he wouldn't have to worry about me.

"All right," Poppy said, sounding lighter. "Um, I'm looking forward to it!"

I smiled. "Me, too, Pops. See ya later."

I hung up and pocketed the phone, then took a deep breath. No matter what happened next, I had to stay positive.

Raising my face to the cool night sky, I imagined the possibilities. I wondered when I'd get the call to return for the Dragonfate Games' third season. Would I meet new friends there? Which dragon would be the next bachelor, and who would be his fated mate?

I shuffled on the balls of my feet. Thinking about love was so exciting, even though I had no experience with it. I'd never even been on a date before. But it still brought me joy to watch my friends Taylor and Matteo fall in love and have adorable babies.

Maybe if I stayed positive, I'd find my true love one day, too.

TWO

Cobalt

THE OCEAN WAVES. The darkening sky. The evening breeze. The shadowy clouds, lit by the pale light of the moon.

All of it coalesced in my soul into an ultimate calm.

My eyes were shut as I stood on the edge of the beach. The cold water lapped at the tips of my boots. Their rhythm was a dance—the waves beckoned me, then pushed me away in an endless cycle.

A soft sigh left my lips. I never tired of the ocean's tranquility. Often, I felt as one with the water, as if my feet would sink into the sand and swallow me whole.

Water was an important part of my hoard. Water was life.

My dragon soul was soothed. He lay just beneath the surface of my skin, a lurking behemoth waiting to breach and sink into the ocean's abyss. We were all one—me, my dragon, and the water.

We were whole. It didn't matter that I was mateless. Childless.

How many times will I tell myself that before I believe it?

The waters of my heart churned with turbulence. My brothers and their children depended on me. The island depended on me, too. They were all my responsibility. Was that not enough?

My dragon's deep, Orphic voice responded, "*No.*"

I sighed. It wasn't often that we were at odds. Since the Dragonfate Games began, my dragon's wants only grew stronger. But the hunger wasn't new. I was the eldest. Longing for my fated mate began when my youngest brothers were barely older than fledglings.

Yet my desires took a backseat to everyone else. There was no other option. I had to protect my family. How could I do that if my loyalties were split between my brothers and my potential mate?

Ignoring my dragon's wordless scolding, I stepped into the salty water. It engulfed my boots. The leather was thin enough that I felt the cold against my skin. That brought me back down to earth.

The tension in my shoulders loosened. Everything was all right. I'd take each day as it came. If fate had chosen a mate for me, all I could do was trust her.

I stood in the tide, allowing the dancing water to calm me.

Then, out of nowhere, a sharp pain struck my heart—an arrowhead ablaze.

My eyes snapped open. I sucked in a ragged breath.

What *was* that? It felt like a knife was lodged in my chest. I couldn't breathe. My heart literally ached.

The sudden pain shattered my tranquility. It provoked my dragon; he reared his head, snarling like a caged bear.

I stared out past the horizon, frozen except for the low growl rumbling in my throat. The sound of it shocked me. I was composed. I was calm. I did not growl unless necessary.

Was this necessary?

What was going on? I didn't understand. Never in my thirty-five years had I experienced such agony. I shook my head, hoping to clear the feeling, but it didn't fade. The arrowhead lodged deeper, rooting itself between my ribs.

"...You listening?"

The voice startled me. Was I so perturbed that I didn't notice somebody sneaking up on me? I turned around slowly, still dazed.

I blew out a breath. It was only my brothers. Crimson and Thystle stood holding Ruby and Heather, respectively. The sight of the young dragonets was a soothing balm on my jittery nerves.

"Hello," I greeted.

Thystle tilted his head towards Crimson. "See? I told you he wasn't listening."

"I can see that," Crimson remarked. He looked like he'd lost a bet. "Are you all right, Cobalt?"

The beautiful dragonets distracted me from the painful sensation in my chest. They squawked cheerfully in greeting. They were so small, so precious. I arched a finger at them playfully and was delighted when they reached for it with tiny claws.

"Cobalt?" Thystle prompted.

"Ah. I'm fine," I said. "What brings you here?"

My amethyst-haired brother sighed. "I mentioned it, but I guess you didn't hear me. We're heading out to see Jade for the meeting."

"Meeting?" I echoed.

Thystle arched a brow. "You know, to decide the next bachelor for the Dragonfate Games?"

Crimson smirked, crossing his arms. "The Games that —if I may be so bold to address—*you* insisted on hosting? Really, Cobalt, if you didn't want to bother with it, you could've sided with me during that argument all those months ago..."

The group meeting. The Games. All of it had slipped my mind. Truth be told, I wasn't in the mood to attend. What use would I be during an important discussion when my heart clenched with peculiar, unknown pain?

Thystle's expression softened. Could he sense my unease? If so, I felt guilty for letting it show. It wasn't my younger brother's duty to worry about me.

"If you don't feel like going, you can just tell us," Thystle said. "Besides, we need a babysitter."

"Taylor and Matteo are having a spa night," Crimson explained before I could ask about their mates.

"What about Viol?" I asked. The surliest of my younger brothers was nasty with us, but nothing but gentle with children. Ever since Ruby hatched, he often volunteered to babysit. Actually, 'volunteered' wasn't the right term. He *demanded* the opportunity to babysit.

Crimson and Thystle exchanged an uneasy glance.

"We don't know where he is," Thystle admitted.

Crimson waved a hand dismissively. "It's not like he attends these meetings, anyway. I suppose it'll be a surprise when his turn comes."

Thystle snorted. "You really want to make *him* the face of the Games? He's gonna get our show cancelled."

"So be it. We can always save him for last," Crimson suggested with a grin.

The mention of Viol made guilt simmer in my belly. What happened to him was my fault. My responsibility. That was why I had to be strict with the others. I wouldn't allow them to be hurt under my watch.

Bored of our adult conversation, the two young dragons swatted their little paws at me, demanding my attention.

I smiled and opened up my broad arms. "I would love to watch them."

"Great!" Crimson unloaded Ruby onto me, then shifted into his sinuous red dragon form.

"We'll come back to fetch them in an hour or two," Thystle said, then followed Crimson's lead. With Heather safely in my arms, he transformed into a spiky purple dragon, and the two of them took off.

I turned back towards the ocean with the little ones in tow. They'd been restless in their fathers' arms, but calmed down in mine. They watched the ebb and flow of the water.

"It's nice, isn't it?" I asked. Pointing up to the moonlit sky, I said, "Look at the clouds. What shapes do you see?"

Ruby and Heather couldn't talk yet, but I knew speaking to infants was important for their development. Plus, I liked to make them feel involved.

Ruby, the older of the two dragonets, shifted to human form and copied my pointing gesture. He jabbed a stubby finger at the cloud drifting lazily overhead. I was surprised to see a familiar shape. The cloud had a spiral shell and two little antennae.

I smiled. "That one looks like a snail. Isn't that nice?"

Not one to be left out, Heather pointed at a different clump of clouds, then looked to me for reassurance.

"Those are wonderful clouds, too," I said. "To me, that one looks like..."

Suddenly, I paused. The cloud was unusually distinct. Its four legs and tail resembled a mammal, and the elongated snout and pointed ears created the iconic silhouette of a fox, or a dog.

I blinked a few times, wondering if I was seeing things, yet the canine cloud remained. Odd.

Out of nowhere, the ache in my chest pulsed. I gritted

my teeth. I didn't want my niece and nephew to see me hurting, so I held steady. I tore my gaze away from the cloud.

"Why don't we hunt for shells on the beach?" I suggested.

Ruby and Heather squealed with excitement as I sat down on the shore. I'd have to apologize to my brothers for the sandy diaper situation later, but for now, the three of us were preoccupied with having fun.

THE NEXT HOUR flew by as we spun fantasies of sand castles, villainous crabs, and seashell warriors. The kids didn't care that it was past their bedtimes—if anything, it fueled them with mischievous energy. Their joyful laughter brightened the evening's darkness, and by the time Crimson and Thystle returned to pick them up, I'd all but forgotten about the mysterious ache in my chest.

The flapping of wings alerted me to their return. The red and purple dragons landed on the sand, then shifted. The kids dropped their shells and crab claws before rushing over to their dads.

Warmth seeped through my chest as Crimson and Thystle hugged their babies. I felt like I'd completed my duty to those two. I raised them to be kind, strong adult men, and now they had families of their own. They were content. Whole. Complete.

The cavity in my heart nagged me. I lowered my face to the sand, then smoothed out the castles and shells, returning them to their natural state. The incoming tide would soon wash the fantasy away, so it felt gentler to do it with my own hands.

"Hey, Cobalt," Crimson called. "Have fun with the rugrats?"

I nodded, concentrating on the sand.

"So, we discussed stuff. At the meeting," Thystle said.

"Mm," I replied.

There was a beat of silence between them.

"Do you... want to know what we talked about?" Thystle prompted.

The meeting was the last thing on my mind. Jade had adopted responsibility for the Games since he enjoyed paperwork and administrative tasks. I wasn't cut out for that sort of thing. I was too distracted. I couldn't crunch numbers and create timetables while protecting my family. What if one of my brothers got hurt while I was in the middle of making a spreadsheet? I'd never forgive myself.

Even now, I worried about Viol. Crimson and Thystle said they couldn't find him. Where had he gone this time? Did he stay on the island?

"Uh, Cobalt?" Thystle asked.

Crimson snorted in amusement. "Good job, big brother. The sand castle has been thoroughly demolished. You truly are a terrifying dragon, through and through."

Terrifying?

I blinked down at the smooth sand, then rose to my feet. I always forgot how much I towered over my brothers until I stood face-to-face with them. They weren't short alphas by any stretch of the imagination, but I received the lion's share of the height genetics. Both my forms were massive.

My size was a double-edged sword. Being big and strong meant I could protect my loved ones, but I also loomed over those same loved ones. I never wanted to intimidate them, or make them uncomfortable. I hoped they looked up to me with trust instead of fear.

"What were we talking about?" I asked.

"The meeting," Crimson said, a grin playing at the corner of his mouth. "Would you like to know what we discussed, or are you content living in blissful ignorance?"

Thystle rolled his eyes. "Shut up, Crimson, we obviously have to tell him."

"Tell me what?" I asked.

Crimson did an exaggerated bow. "You, my dearest older brother, are the next bachelor of the Dragonfate Games."

I stared at him blankly. "I am?"

Thystle nodded. "That's what we all decided."

I didn't understand. Most of my younger brothers had yet to have their turn in the spotlight. It made no sense for me to skip the line.

"Why me?" I questioned.

"Why *not* you?" Thystle countered. "You deserve a mate, just like the rest of us."

I furrowed my brow. That was true, but I didn't need my younger brother to worry about my love life. That was my job.

Since I took too long to formulate a decent argument, they took my silence as acceptance.

"Great! You're on for season three," Crimson announced. "I'm excited to see how this shakes out. Oh, *please* let me pick an outfit for you. You cannot go on television wearing a T-shirt and jeans."

"What's wrong with that?" Thystle grumbled.

Crimson shuddered. "Everything."

I closed my mouth, my half-baked argument dying on my lips. The decision was already made for me. I was going to be the next bachelor of the Dragonfate Games. Omegas would flock to the island to meet me—and if I was lucky, one of them would be my fated mate.

Without thinking, I lifted my head to the night sky. The dog-shaped cloud was still floating above the moon, almost playful in its lazy speed.

I couldn't take my eyes off it.

THREE

Muzo

"ZAVALA!"

I winced. The way Bobby barked my last name made him feel more like a drill sergeant than a manager at a fast food restaurant.

"One sec," I called back.

Grilling burgers was serious work. They had to be flipped at a precise time for the perfect char, all while *not* splashing myself with hot oil. It took my full focus. I didn't want a customer to get a sub-par burger because Bobby needed to chat.

"No, not one second, now!" Bobby snarled.

I bit my lip. I counted down the cooking time in my head, but Bobby's yelling ruined my concentration. I lost track of the seconds.

"Uh," I said, glancing over my shoulder. Bobby stood at the end of the kitchen with his arms crossed. He tapped his foot impatiently in a 'get over here now' gesture.

But the burger needed me. I looked back down to the grill, my trusty spatula at the ready. Was it ten seconds left, or thirty? Damn it. I wished he'd just come to my station to talk instead of pulling me away from my work.

In the end, I chose the burger. I didn't want to disappoint the customer. Sneaking the edge of the spatula under the burger, I checked the char situation. It was done, but a couple more seconds would've been perfect...

"Muzo Zavala," Bobby roared over the kitchen's chaos. "If you don't get your butt over here right now, you're fired!"

Well, that just wasn't fair.

Hoping one of my coworkers would save my poor burger from being burnt to a crisp, I put the spatula down and hurried over to him.

"Yes, Bobby?" I asked urgently. "I've got a burger on the grill, so—"

Bobby leaned in closer, squinting hard. He took a couple sniffs, then recoiled with a disgusted sound.

"God, you reek!"

"Huh?"

I sniffed myself. I smelled normal—to my nose, anyway, and I knew I had a keener sense of smell than a human.

Well, okay, *maybe* I had a stronger scent than usual. I spent last night on the street and I had no place to shower, but that didn't mean I was dirty. I licked myself clean in jackal form and took a dip in the local river in human form. Plus, I had the power of deodorant on my side. I couldn't smell *that* bad.

Bobby didn't agree. His nose wrinkled like he'd just opened a Dumpster.

"You stink like a dog," Bobby blurted out.

The tips of my ears felt hot with embarrassment. If I'd been in my jackal form, my tail would've slipped between my legs. But I guess it was better to be in human form right now. If Bobby thought I smelled like a dog while I stood on two legs, he'd lose it if I was on four...

"I'm sorry," I said, bowing my head.

Like my ex-superintendent George, Bobby also knew I was a shifter. I couldn't help but volunteer that information whenever people asked. In the past, I'd done the whole song and dance of hiding my shifter identity. It never worked out. Besides, I wasn't ashamed, so why hide it?

Bobby gestured wildly with his hands as he spoke. "Listen, I know you're a transformer or whatever they're called, but food service has a strict *no animals* policy. You can't be getting dog hair or dander or *smell* on the food."

I winced. Bobby's brutal honesty sucked to hear. It wasn't like I flipped burgers with my paws and shook out my pelt all over the grill. I was in human form, just like all the other actual humans working here.

"I'm really sorry. I'll fix it right after my shift, I swear," I insisted.

How was I gonna fix it exactly? I had no clue. But I'd figure something out. I always did.

"You'd better." Bobby pinched his nose. "Man, you smell worse than my Labrador retriever after he jumps in the pool..."

I stood there awkwardly. It was always weird when humans compared us to their actual, non-shifter pets.

"Take a bath tonight. Got it?" Bobby demanded.

I nodded vigorously. "Yeah, definitely. Except, uh..."

One of Bobby's brows ran for his hairline. "What?"

What could I say? Should I lie? I didn't wanna do that. It was hard enough dodging the truth with Poppy the other day. Maybe Bobby would be more sympathetic towards me if he knew I'd been evicted.

I stammered. "It's actually—well, what happened is—er, the concept of a bath really changes from person to person, doesn't it—"

"Spit it out, Zavala," Bobby barked.

I sighed. "I lost my apartment. So, I can't really take a bath. Or a shower. Not in an actual shower or bathtub, anyway."

Bobby's face paled. Was he imagining my plight? I took that as a good sign. My sympathy strategy was working!

"Oh, also," I continued, "since I don't technically have an address anymore, could I get my next paycheck in cash instead of mailed to my apartment?"

Bobby groaned and rubbed his temples. The next words out of his mouth sideswiped me.

"Pack up your stuff, Muzo," Bobby ordered. "Sorry, but you're outta here."

I stared at him in shock. "Huh?"

Bobby shook his head. "Look, I know it's rough, but we can't have you workin' here no more. If you can't keep clean, it's gonna be an ongoing issue. Can't have unhygienic staff in the kitchen. Sorry."

I realized that I misunderstood Bobby's expression. He didn't have empathy for me. He had pity, like I was some kind of charity case he'd just condemned. It was weird, and I didn't like it. The repugnance he felt towards me was a thousand times worse than getting fired.

"Okay," I said, because what else could I say? I glanced back at the grill. To add insult to injury, my burger was half charcoal. "Um, about my last burger..."

Bobby waved his hand. "Just take it with you." He fished out his wallet, pulled out a twenty, and thrust it at me like he was paying off a problem. "Here's your paycheck. See ya."

I didn't stick around long. I said goodbye to my coworkers and the grill, grabbed the blackened burger patty, then left.

Hey, at least I got twenty bucks and a meal.

For the second night in a row, I sat alone on a curb outside of a place that just told me to get lost. I munched on my charred burger. It was pretty good, burnt bits and all.

What could I do with the twenty? Since I had no more bills to pay, the sky was the limit. Well, twenty dollars was the limit. I could go to the dollar store and buy twenty things. But then where would I put them? My luggage was already full of clothes and toiletries, so they'd have to fit in my bag.

I took another bite, chewing slowly. My mind drifted to Chromatimaeus Island and the alpha dragons living there. In hindsight, their generosity was incredible. They'd fed us, housed us, paid for our flights and all travel expenses. All we had to do was show up. I felt lucky to be part of the first two seasons, and now an upcoming third.

Four months had passed since season two ended, when Thystle and Matteo found each other. The show had hit the ground running, and its popularity exploded with the second season.

But the most important thing was that my friends were happy. Taylor lost his grumpy edge when he fell in love with Crimson, and Thystle pulled Matteo out of his secret identity crisis. Both couples were perfect for each other.

I swallowed the last bite of my charred burger, then sighed wistfully. Being fated to a dragon sounded awesome.

My stomach growled. Even though my shift was cut short, it was a long one, and I was still hungry after devouring the patty.

Just as I thought about rummaging through garbage cans, I saw a familiar white-haired figure walking towards me.

"Poppy!" I greeted, leaping up from the curb.

He flashed a shy smile. "Hi," he said softly, fidgeting with his backpack strap. "I brought the cookies."

I gasped happily. With everything going on, the cookies slipped my mind.

"Pops, you're amazing!" I cried.

A blush tinged his pale cheeks. "N-no, I'm not. They're just cookies."

"Uh, no. They're Poppy's Most Epic Cookies Ever."

He huffed gently, then pulled a package out of his bag. The environmentally friendly wrapper was made of beeswax and cotton, and had cute little flowers on it.

He offered it to me. "Here you go. They're not as fresh as they were yesterday, but..."

The package was hefty. There had to be at least ten cookies in there. Talk about a decent meal.

I grinned. "You know I love a little staleness in my cookies. Thanks, Poppy. You're the best."

Praise always made Poppy squirm, like he thought he didn't deserve it.

I put the cookies in my bag to save them for later. If I scarfed them all down now, I'd regret it when I got hungry.

Poppy tilted his head curiously. "You're not going to try one?"

Crap. I usually *did* eat one right away.

Maybe one wouldn't hurt. I didn't want Poppy to get suspicious. I grabbed one from the wrapper and took a slow bite, savoring the flavor.

"Mmm... See? Epic," I said.

He smiled shyly. That seemed to calm his anxiety.

"Um, how was your shift?" he asked.

I shrugged as I took another bite. "Fine. Same as usual."

The words felt gross as they slipped out of me. Lying to

Poppy was like pouring a bucket of water on a rain-soaked kitten.

"That's good," Poppy replied.

"Yup," I agreed.

I kept chewing. Poppy didn't make a move to leave. Now what?

I bounced on the balls of my feet. "Well... I better head home. Big day and all. Thanks for the grub, Pops."

"Sure." Poppy paused, then suddenly sniffed the air. "Um..."

I froze. Crap.

Poppy was a wolf shifter. His nose was infinitely better than a human's. There was no doubt he noticed my heightened I-haven't-had-a-real-shower-for-two-days smell. Would he ask why?

But Poppy also had debilitating anxiety. Maybe he'd be too nervous to bring it up for fear of offending me.

Poppy bit his lip. "Um... Muzo—"

My phone suddenly rang.

Poppy yelped, nearly jumping out of his skin. I was grateful for the interruption. It saved me from a gnarly game of trying not to lie to my best friend.

I picked up the call without checking the caller ID. "Yo!"

"Hi Muzo!" Winnie's familiar voice replied.

Excitement bloomed in my chest. Winnie was the dragons' secretary. She only ever called about the Dragonfate Games.

"I bet you've already guessed what this call is about," Winnie remarked.

"The Games?" I asked eagerly.

Beside me, Poppy gasped, his brown eyes widening.

"Oh, I recognize that little baby voice. Is Poppy with you?" Winnie asked.

"Sure is," I confirmed.

"Great! That saves me another phone call." Winnie cleared her throat. "Pack your bags, boys! Dragonfate Games season three! Be there or be square! No, but seriously, your flights are booked for next Friday. We'll send the cabs to your addresses as usual. See you soon!"

FOUR

Cobalt

_____

VOICES SURROUNDED me as Jade and Duke hashed out details of the upcoming television season. I was present for the discussion, but only physically. I wasn't really here. My mind was elsewhere.

I stared out into the horizon from the bay window in Jade's office. It was in a separate room from the personal library that was his hoard, the architectural equivalent of a mudroom separating us from his precious books. I had more leeway to be close to Jade's hoard, since I was his eldest brother, but Duke had no such privilege.

Though I couldn't say I afforded my brothers the same courtesy. None of them had ever seen my hoard—or even knew its contents. That was a secret I held close to my chest.

Dragons were selfish when it came to our hoards. It was an indisputable fact of our nature.

Unlike us, Duke was a kobold. He had reptilian features, but was short and stout, smaller than even a human. And similar to humans, he didn't understand the gravity of a dragon's hoard. He grumbled about being 'stuffed' into Jade's office, but his complaints were quickly silenced by an uncharacteristically menacing glare from Jade.

The meeting went smoother after that.

"Now, let's discuss the challenges," Jade said with a polite smile. "We've had issues in the past where the contestants and bachelors felt the challenges didn't suit their needs, so let's correct them moving forward."

I rested my chin on my hand as I gazed out into the horizon. The clouds were moving again. As the sun descended towards the water, it cast romantic hues of pink and violet across the clouds. They resembled floating bits of cotton candy. Sweet and airy and light.

"So, what would you prefer?" Jade asked. "Challenges that cater to the omegas' physical prowess? Ones that showcase their intelligence and problem-solving skills? Something else entirely? I'm all ears."

Remembering to respond was a feat.

"Yes... No. Maybe," I mumbled without looking at him.

"Yes, no, maybe what?" Jade prompted.

I'd already lost my train of thought. "Sorry, what was the question?"

Duke made a frustrated sound. "He's too damn busy daydreamin' over there to listen!"

As I watched the clouds shift, the kobold's complaint melted into the background. I sat up straighter, watching the cotton-candy puffs elongate and grow. They almost formed a shape. One I'd seen somewhere before.

My eyes widened as the clouds stretched into four legs, a sharp snout, and pointed ears.

There he was again—my little canine friend.

Someone put their hand on my arm. I whirled. If it was Duke, I would've growled at him, but it was only my brother. The tension in my muscles stilled. I never snarled at family.

Jade smiled patiently. There was trust in his expression. He knew I wouldn't have snapped at him.

"If you don't want to do this right now, we can reschedule," he suggested. "But it's a discussion we need to have together."

I sighed. "I know..."

"What's on your mind? You're unusually preoccupied."

I glanced over my shoulder at the distant clouds. How could I explain the welling of emotion in my chest when I saw them? Every time I tried to string the right words together, they dissipated like mist. It was impossible.

"Sorry," I said.

"It's all right," Jade replied gently. "If you're not feeling creative right now, I'll bounce ideas off you instead. You can approve or disapprove accordingly."

"Okay."

I itched to turn towards the window again, but Jade held my gaze. His green eyes were steady and assured. Whenever I saw the confident, smart way he carried himself, it filled me with pride. What a fine dragon I raised.

"We all want this to be a pleasant experience for you," Jade said. "You're our big brother. We *want* you to find your mate. You deserve it."

My throat tightened with emotion. Just when I thought I couldn't be more proud. But it was hard for me to show it. I was my family's anchor, a composed constant in their lives. If I let my feelings run wild, who would be their rock?

I couldn't think of the right words, so I nodded instead.

That was enough for Jade. He picked up his meticulous stack of papers and said, "Well then. I've got a few ideas to share..."

THE REST of the meeting passed without fanfare, or much input from me. The clouds stole my attention. I couldn't recall anything I'd said, so the Dragonfate Games would be a surprise.

As the dying sun painted dramatic colors across the ocean, the canine-shaped cloud remained in the same spot. It hadn't gone anywhere. The two hours I'd spent in Jade's office meant nothing to the loyal cotton-candy creature. It floated close to the ocean's surface, like its paws were skimming the water. I couldn't take my eyes off it.

What was it? What did it mean?

The arrow in my heart pulsed with a deep ache. I grunted, slapping my hand across my chest. Would this keep happening during the Games? If it was a medical issue, perhaps I could avoid the Games entirely.

But that meant admitting I needed help, and that was one thing I couldn't do. No, I couldn't tell anybody about the ache in my chest—especially not my brothers. I would weather this trial on my own, just like I always did.

Still clutching my chest, I faced the horizon. To my odd disappointment, the dog-shaped cloud was gone.

It was only a cloud, I told myself. They came and went. It was their nature.

Instead, I focused on the water. The far-off waves flowed rhythmically. Their existence usually calmed me, but something was different. It looked like something was *in* the water—trapped in the ocean current, being pushed and pulled in every direction, unable to break free.

Was somebody drowning?

The pain in my chest flared. Whoever it was, I had to save them.

My behemoth dragon tore free from the shackles of my

human form. Pumping my wings, I flew towards the shape. Was it my imagination, or did it resemble the dog-shaped cloud? Panic flooded me.

I'll save you, I promised silently.

I cursed my huge dragon body. We grew with age, and as the eldest, I was the biggest of us all. But my gargantuan size burdened me with weak agility. Would I be fast enough to save the drowning creature?

When I finally reached the turbulent waves, I banked my wings and stopped. I scanned the water frantically, but saw nothing. Where was it? Had it already gone under?

My mind went blank. I didn't think—I only reacted.

I dove under the waves, snapping my eyes wide open. But where I'd expected to see a figure, a body, anything... there was nothing. Only water.

Had I daydreamed the canine shape in the ocean? Did I trick myself into believing it was there?

A strange mixture of feelings swirled inside me. Disappointment, relief, and emptiness.

I breached the surface and shot up into the sky. I wasn't ready to return to my human form. Now that my dragon was free, he refused to be shoved back into a body based on logical thought. He thrived on instinct alone.

And his instinct was to fly.

To escape the island.

To go find... something.

Someone.

My mind went blank. The water beneath me rippled as the leathery snap of my massive wings propelled me forward. The urge to find my mate burned in my blood. I didn't know who they were, but I sensed a great chasm of distance between us. I closed my eyes as the mental image formed in my mind.

They were on the other side of the water. On land, surrounded by sprawling architecture. The human city.

The place where—except in extreme circumstances—I'd forbidden my younger brothers to go.

But I was different. I was the eldest. If instinct summoned me to the city, I had to follow.

A sudden impact slammed into me. I spiralled, my balance thrown off. My eyes snapped open and my wings flapped wildly in an attempt to right myself. That collision was too large and precise to be anything but another dragon.

I looped around to confront the offender—and came face-to-face with the deep purple scales of my brother Viol.

"Fancy meeting you here," he growled.

I was speechless, partly because of my shock, but also because I was deeply relieved to see him. I'd been worried ever since Crimson and Thystle said he was missing.

"Where have you been?" I asked.

He snorted out a derisive puff of smoke. "None of your fucking business. Now, let me ask *you* something." He darted around me in a half-circle, blocking my path. "Where the hell do you think you're going?"

The question caught me off-guard. I hovered, slowly beating my wings.

"To the city," I replied.

Viol barked out a cutting, humorless laugh. "No."

That wasn't what I expected.

I made the rules, and my brothers followed them. The staff we hired all listened to my orders without question. I wasn't used to being told 'no.'

"What do you mean?" I asked, genuinely confused.

Viol's eyes blazed as he stared back at me. "I said no.

That's it. I'm not letting you fly out of our territory all alone."

Nothing but ocean surrounded us. I couldn't see Chromatimaeus Island, not even as a tiny speck in the distance. How far had I flown without realizing it? I must've been deep in the haze of my instincts.

I turned back to Viol. The urge to fly still consumed me, except now my own brother was an obstacle in my path.

"You don't make the rules," I said.

"No. *You* do. So, follow them," he snapped. "Stay on the fucking island where it's safe."

Was he... worried about me? He wasn't supposed to do that. It was my job to bear that burden.

"I won't get into trouble," I promised, hoping it was enough to assuage his concerns.

Instead, he cackled bitterly. "Oh, really? You won't? Look at you, Cobalt. You're a dragon the size of a small country. You're a fucking *behemoth*. You'll find trouble wherever you go. Except at home. Go back and stay there."

I was speechless. I'd been confronted by my brothers before when they fought for something they believed in. When Thystle wanted to attend a concert as a teenager, claiming fervently that his fated mate was there, I'd asked him to prove his resolve. I still had the scars on my arm as evidence of his rightful win.

But Viol didn't want anything from me. He just wanted me to stay home. Stay safe.

In a way, I felt like I'd failed him again. I was Cobalt, the eldest alpha dragon. I was untouchable. My family didn't need to worry over me, least of all Viol.

When I didn't respond, Viol curled his lip to reveal a sneering row of fangs. "Let me guess. You *need* to go."

"That is how I feel," I said simply. As a reminder, I added, "Thystle was allowed to leave the island."

"But he didn't," Viol countered. "And if shit went down differently and he *did* try to leave, I would've stopped his ass, too."

He was beyond fired up. He was furious. I hadn't realized Viol felt so strongly about this. But perhaps I shouldn't have been surprised, given his turbulent past.

"It's about your fated mate, isn't it?" Viol asked. There was no sympathy or gentleness in his tone. It was as sharp and cold as a knife.

My breath hitched.

My fated mate. Could that be what all this was about? I brought my claws to my broad chest where the ache still lingered.

"I don't know," I said honestly.

Viol shook his head and let out a disparaging grunt. "You don't even fucking know." Narrowing his dark purple eyes, he snapped his wings and drew closer to me. "Throw your life away for a hunch, why don't you? That's a real smart idea. I can't fucking believe you almost let Thystle do the same thing. I'm still pissed at you about that, but whatever."

"Viol," I murmured. I had no idea he felt that way. He never spoke openly about his emotions. He was too guarded, a cornered cat with all its claws out.

"I'll fight you, Cobalt," Viol warned. His eyes flashed. He was serious. "Step past me and see what happens. Because I am *not* letting anything bad happen to you."

A different dragon might've been furious at Viol's defiance. He could rake Viol across the face with his claws, bite his throat until he submitted, and order that he never oppose him again.

But I was a true alpha. I was a guardian, a caretaker,

and above all, the protector to everyone I held dear. To see my brother in such a state didn't fill me with rage; it saddened me. I only wanted him to be happy.

"All right," I said quietly.

Viol blinked, then furrowed his scaly brow. "What?"

Banking my wings, I slowly turned my large body around. Viol was smaller and faster. He caught up with me in a heartbeat.

"You're not angry?" he demanded.

"Viol," I said, looking at him. "When have I ever been angry with you?"

Chaotic emotions flickered in his eyes. He quickly put up his wing like a wall between us so I couldn't see his face.

His voice was thick as he muttered, "You're so fucking..." He let out a sharp sigh. "Listen. I don't control you. Just wait a little longer. If your fated mate's out there, he might be a contestant in the next Games. Right?"

That hadn't even crossed my mind. I'd been so distracted recently, I couldn't see the bigger picture.

"Oh," I said. "Yes. That's possible."

Viol sounded relieved. "Okay. And if he's not, then... live your fucking life."

I thought I heard a hint of embarrassment in Viol's tone. He pumped his wings hard, then exploded upwards into the sky, disappearing behind the vibrant clouds.

I flew back home like Viol insisted. But I couldn't help glancing over my shoulder at the possibilities beyond the horizon.

Was my fated mate really out there?

And if so, was he the source of this ache in my chest?

FIVE

Muzo

TODAY WAS THE BIG DAY. My flight to Chromatimaeus Island for the third Dragonfate Games was scheduled for this afternoon.

And instead of wasting time sitting in the fancy lounge, I was doing something way more important—hunting for breakfast.

Since I had nothing better to do, I arrived at the private airport early. Poppy's cookies and my last twenty bucks ran out a couple days ago, so I resorted to doing things the old-fashioned way.

Outside the building, I put my clothes in a pile beside the Dumpster, then shifted. I prowled around in my jackal form. The trash zone was the hotspot—where there was garbage, there were rodents. Yum.

My ears pricked at the sound of high-pitched squeaking. It was my lucky day. A big, juicy rat licked itself on top of a cardboard box nearby.

I pressed my belly low to the ground and licked my lips. The last time I'd eaten was two days ago, and that was only a measly mouse with a side of discarded ketchup-smeared

BurgerMart wrapper. Compared to that, this rat was a feast.

"Come to papa," I murmured.

The rat stopped.

Crap. It heard me.

Why did I say that out loud?

It was now or never. Throwing caution to the wind, I launched myself at the rat. But my prey was tougher than it looked. Instead of running away, it reared angrily and sunk its teeth into my snout.

Pain exploded through my nerves. I howled in agony, throwing myself on the ground and rolling around to dislodge the rat. It jumped free and ran on top of the Dumpster, glaring at me. I couldn't tell if I was seeing things because of the tears blurring my vision, or if the rat was giving me the finger.

I sniffled, lying my head on my paws. It was fine. I mean, the pain throbbing in my snout royally sucked, but it was okay because soon I'd be on the plane to Chromatimaeus Island. Once I was there, I could eat and shower and do all that nice stuff.

Well, until the Games ended again. Then I'd have to come back 'home.'

And if I didn't find my mate this time, I'd have no home to return to.

One thing was clear: if this was my life now, then I needed to improve my rat hunting skills ASAP.

"Dear gods," a voice muttered behind me, accompanied by a familiar baby powder scent. "Zavala, is that you?"

I yelped in surprise, jumping a foot in the air and landing on all four paws. A white-haired omega stared down at me with disdain. Or concern. Or both.

"Alaric!" I cried.

He scrutinized me with his odd-colored eyes. "What the hell happened to you? You're absolutely filthy."

I heard that a lot lately. Was it getting worse? I glanced down at my fur. It was usually coarse but clean. Now it was greasy, dull, and weirdly sticky in certain areas. I'd been so busy trying to find food that I'd forgotten to wash my coat.

I shamefully tucked my paws beneath me. "I know..."

"Why?" Alaric asked. He was flabbergasted, like he couldn't possibly imagine having more than a single speck of dust on him.

"It's, er, a long story," I replied.

Alaric blinked at me incredulously. My pitiful appearance seemed to throw a wrench in his sassy attitude, rendering him speechless.

After a long moment, Alaric pinched the bridge of his nose and exhaled. "Let me get this straight. We've got a flight in—" He checked his expensive-looking watch. "Two hours. And you're outside sitting in garbage."

"Technically, I'm *standing* in garbage."

"For the love of..." Alaric huffed, making a curt hand gesture. "Does it matter, Muzo? You're dirty, and you reek of wet dog and trash."

I perked up with a grin. That was the first time Alaric had ever addressed me by name instead of 'dog,' 'jackal,' or 'hey, you.' He must've been pretty worried about me.

"What are you smiling about?" Alaric demanded. "Have you lost what few brain cells you had rattling around in that little head of yours?"

"My head's average-sized. I think."

Alaric made a frustrated sound. "Just... wait here. And stop chasing rats. You're the furthest thing from a competent hunter. Next time, it's going to bite your nose clean off."

My ears flattened. That sounded horrifying. I nervously

eyed the rat from earlier, who still reigned as the king of the Dumpster.

"Okay," I mumbled.

Alaric stormed off in a tizzy. I forgot to ask where he was going, but in case he planned on coming back, I figured I'd stay put.

I sat down next to the Dumpster. My stomach growled. I was really looking forward to the in-flight meal. Last time, I ordered my favorite food, grilled shrimp. It even came with a side of cream sauce. My mouth filled with saliva just thinking about it...

A loud gasp tore me from my food daydream.

"Muzo!" Poppy cried.

Oh no.

My heart plummeted to the pit of my stomach. I wanted to avoid Poppy until we reached the hotel and I got my shit together, but that was naive. He was my best friend, and we'd be on the same flight. Surely he'd sniff me out and cling to my side sooner or later.

I didn't want him to see me like this. I'd wormed my way out of explaining it the last two times we spoke, but now that I was a certified trash-dweller, there was no way he'd believe the 'everything is A-okay!' story.

Poppy ran towards me, his big doe eyes wide with concern. Alaric stood behind him with his arms crossed and brows knitted. He must've fetched Poppy from the airport lounge when he saw what a sorry state I was in. Man, what a commotion I'd caused.

"Muzo, what happened?" Poppy asked, his voice raising in pitch. He sounded like he was about to cry.

Guilt wormed its way through my insides. The last thing I ever wanted to do was make Poppy cry.

"Hey, it's okay," I said, wagging my tail to calm him.

"Your pelt is—it's—it's so dirty!" Poppy wailed. Unlike Alaric, there was no contempt in his voice.

Trying to keep my tone light, I said, "Yeah, I know. It's fine."

Poppy bit his lip. I practically saw the internal war waging in his mind—should he obediently take my word for it, or argue with me?

Shockingly, he picked the latter.

"You know what? No, it's not fine," Poppy insisted. "You look terrible. Hang on."

He checked over his shoulder to make sure no humans were present, then quickly discarded his clothes and shifted into his arctic wolf form. His tongue flew across my fur, licking me as thoroughly and aggressively as a parent who'd just given birth to pups.

"Poppy, come on," I said. "I'm—pffbt."

He cut me off as his tongue cleaned my dirty snout, including the blood from the rat bite. Within seconds, I was damp with warm wolf slobber.

Alaric let out a disdainful sigh. "Dogs."

"Hey, you lick yourself, too, *cat*," I shot back.

"I'm also familiar with the concept of shampoo," Alaric said dryly.

"Me too. I just can't afford it."

Poppy stopped suddenly. "What did you say?"

Crap.

"Uh... I can't afford... time to go to the store?"

Poppy's brown eyes bore into me gravely. "Muzo."

"Oh dear," Alaric remarked. "Am I about to witness a lover's quarrel?"

I snorted. "We're not lovers, we're friends. Y'know, 'cause some of us actually have them."

That was a mean thing to say, but I was super overwhelmed. I was annoyed at myself for getting Poppy involved—and honestly, Alaric too. I should've done a better job keeping my problems a secret.

Alaric didn't sound offended. He examined his nails. "Some of us also don't have a twelve-mile stink radius."

Before I could respond, Poppy headbutted my cheek to get my attention.

"Muzo, tell me what's really going on." His soft voice had a serious edge, one I didn't hear often.

I could lie, but what could I possibly say that would sound plausible? And did I really want to lie? It wouldn't help—Poppy was already distraught, and Alaric had watched me lose a fight to a rat. There wasn't any lower I could go.

"So... I lost my job," I began.

Poppy let out a sympathetic gasp.

"And my apartment," I continued.

His jaw hung open. "*What?*"

"And your dignity," Alaric mumbled. He sounded serious, not like he was making fun of me.

"Yup, pretty much," I agreed. "But other than that, I'm fine! Look, I've got all four paws and my head on straight. So don't worry about me, okay?"

Poppy swayed like he was going to faint.

I pressed against him for support. "Hey, c'mon, it's not that bad, Pops. We're about to go to the Dragonfate Games! I'll get cleaned up and fed, and everything will be okay."

"The Games," Poppy murmured, then perked up. "Right, the Dragonfate Games. Taylor will be there. I need to tell him."

"No," I blurted out.

Poppy and Alaric both stared at me like I'd lost it. But I

hadn't. Taylor had his own life and his own responsibilities. It wasn't fair to disrupt his perfect existence with my own personal problems. I was a grown man. I could take care of myself.

"Don't tell Taylor," I urged. "He's got enough to worry about. He's a parent with a kid, remember? I don't need him to babysit me."

Poppy's brow furrowed in concern. "But—"

"Please, Poppy. Don't tell anyone. This is important to me. I want to fix this on my own."

How? I didn't know yet. But I'd figure something out. I always did.

Poppy fussed and whimpered. He looked like he wanted to grab me by the scruff and carry me around like a pup. But I didn't want that—at least, not from him.

I wouldn't mind it so much coming from a dragon.

Wait, why was I thinking about dragons?

I shook it off. "Promise?"

Poppy's tail lay flat and listless on the ground. He wasn't happy about this.

"Promise?" I asked again.

"Okay. I promise," he murmured, hanging his head.

I wagged my tail. "Thanks. I'll fix everything, don't you worry. Just trust me, okay?"

Poppy nodded, but his expression was plagued with anxiety. I kept a positive attitude for his sake. I bounced up on all fours and gathered my clothes.

"Thanks for the bath, Pops," I said before shifting to human form. "I smell a lot better already!"

"Debatable," Alaric said, raising a brow. He suddenly reached into his pocket, pulled out a weird perfume bottle, then spritzed me with it before I could refuse.

"Hey!" I cried. Beside me, Poppy sneezed.

"It was for your own good, and for the sake of everybody on the plane," Alaric said primly, pocketing the bottle like a smoking gun. "You should be thanking me. That was *very* expensive cologne."

I sniffed my shirt, then groaned. "Great. Now I smell like a freshly powdered baby butt."

SIX

Cobalt
_____

"...AND good luck on the third season of the Dragonfate Games!"

As Gaius finished the opening ceremony, dozens of voices cheered in excitement. I glanced at the rows of unfamiliar omegas below the platform. They blended together in a faceless mass. I felt nothing towards them. Most would go home disappointed.

But one thing had changed.

The arrow lodged in my ribs shifted.

I clutched my chest absentmindedly, running my fingers over the low ache. It was an antithetical feeling. It had settled, yet also intensified—like it was muted, yet put on full volume at the same time.

Was Viol right? Was my fated mate here in this crowd?

I scanned the faces again. The men varied in every-thing—age, height, weight, skin color. Some were so tall that they blocked the omegas behind them. There was one in particular I couldn't quite see...

"You all right, big boss?"

Gaius looped his arm around my shoulder—or at least,

he tried to. Like most people, he wasn't quite tall enough to reach, so he patted my shoulder blades instead.

"Sorry?" I said.

Gaius noticed my splintered attention. He wriggled his brows. "Ah, seduced by the crowd already?"

"No."

Gaius sighed, shaking his head. "I'm waiting for one of you dragons to be *excited* about being a bachelor. Aren't you all about hoarding?" He mimed collecting an armful of invisible objects. "What's more fun than omegas on each arm?"

I frowned. "We only hoard what we love. That includes our mate."

"Yes, yes, I know. Besides, I can't see you as the playboy type." Flashing a devilish grin, Gaius added under his breath, "Unless you have a naughty side I don't know about."

"I don't," I said bluntly.

He nodded. "Ah well. You're as honest as a brick wall."

I suddenly remembered the omegas. I turned around, but they were gone. The staff had already escorted them back to their hotel rooms. The ache in my chest flared.

"I have to go," I said, stepping off the platform.

Gaius leapt off behind me. "Er, Cobalt, you're not heading for the hotel, are you?" he stage-whispered.

I nodded brusquely.

"Well, *I* have no problem with a little harmless rule-breaking, but technically you're not *supposed* to visit the omegas in their hotel rooms, especially not in broad daylight—"

The show. I'd forgotten.

But it didn't matter. Not when he was so close.

Nothing was getting in my way now.

I ripped the mic attachment from my shirt and handed it to a baffled Gaius.

"Cobalt?" he squawked. "What are you——"

"Give it back to me later," I instructed.

Then I walked straight into the hotel.

I HAD NEVER BEEN inside the building before. When we first discussed the concept of the Games, I agreed to build a lavish modern hotel for our omega guests, but Jade and the staff took care of the rest. It never crossed my mind. Until this moment, it had been just another building on our territory.

Now it was an extravagant labyrinth that stood between me and my mate.

People scurried about around me—various shifter omegas and scaly little kobolds. Some were hotel staff, some were camera crew. I took extra care not to bump into the kobolds. They were so short that I only noticed them when I looked down.

I scanned the lobby. Not all the shifter omegas were here. The others must have returned to their rooms. I didn't recognize any of them, but they stared at me with wide-eyed wonder.

Should I smile and wave? I was busy, but it wouldn't hurt to be polite. I raised a hand in greeting. Some of them swooned.

I instantly regretted waving.

As I continued on my way, I heard their ecstatic voices behind me: "Guys, Cobalt looked at me! He actually looked at me and waved!"

The hallway full of elated squeals faded into the background as I climbed the stairs. What floor was he on? Which room? Each door I passed made my heart thud faster, made the arrow pulse harder.

I was close. I felt it.

My feet suddenly stopped on their own. A door stood before me. It looked the same as any other hotel door, but this one was different.

My mate was behind this door. I knew it.

Inside my soul, my dragon rumbled, looping in circles impatiently.

Open the door, he demanded.

I grabbed the handle. The electronic key card reader flashed red and made a quiet error sound.

I frowned. First it was Viol, and now a hotel door told me 'no,' too.

But this time, I wasn't taking no for an answer.

My knuckles went white as I curled my fingers around the handle. Hidden power flowed through my body. I breathed deeply, then wrenched my arm back.

A loud *crack* echoed in the hall.

I yanked the entire door off its hinges.

Keen gasps sounded behind me, along with the shuffling feet of camera crew kobolds. When had all these people shown up?

A rectangular hole remained where the door had been seconds earlier, and through this new window, I saw a short, bewildered man and his naked bottom.

And so would everybody else crowded in the hallway, if I wasn't so big that I blocked their view.

My dragon growled in a mix of satisfaction and jealousy. I wanted no one else to witness this man's nakedness.

In a smooth motion, I stepped into the room and deposited the door back in place behind me. It wasn't perfect, but at least the man's nude body wasn't on full display anymore.

The naked omega blinked at me in silence, so I seized the opportunity to examine him.

The first thing I noticed was his tiny size. He was short and wiry, easily small enough to pick up with one arm. His eyes were dark brown, bordering on black, and his skin was a warm shade of brown. His hair was sandy blond, edged with black tips, which I suspected was natural. It reminded me of a certain animal's pelt color. It reminded me of—

I sucked in a breath, frozen to the spot.

I *knew* this omega. He was a black-backed jackal shifter, and he'd been a contestant on the Dragonfate Games twice before.

A sudden wave of guilt slammed into me. Until now, I hadn't paid attention to any of the contestants. My mind was preoccupied with protecting my family. I didn't think I was ready—or perhaps worthy—to find a mate of my own.

But now this naked jackal shifter stood before me, and the agonizing pain in my chest finally dissolved.

He was home. Right where I wanted him.

Now if I could only remember his name.

A minute had passed, and still neither of us had spoken. As the host and the alpha, it was my responsibility to go first.

"Sorry for the intrusion," I said, bowing my head.

The naked omega stared.

He could've screamed at me to get lost. Even if we were fated mates, that was fully within his right. He'd just arrived at the hotel, and already I'd broken in his door and shattered his privacy.

Instead, he burst into bright laughter. It rang in my ears like music, and a shiver shot down my spine.

"You're... not mad?" I asked.

The omega grinned and wiped a joyful tear from his eye. "No way. That was so freaking funny. Man, I needed a good laugh."

My mouth curved into a smile. His grin was as compelling as his laughter. It bloomed across his face, lighting up his whole being.

Who *was* this omega? Why had I never paid attention to him before? Guilt filled the hole where the arrowhead's ache had been. Had I seen him during the first two closing ceremonies, or had his tiny self always been buried behind a sea of taller faces?

"So, uh," the omega began, bouncing on the balls of his feet. His bare feet. "You often barge into naked guys' rooms unannounced?"

He sounded amused, not accusatory.

"No," I said honestly. "Just you."

His bouncing paused and his dark eyes widened before he broke into a lopsided grin. "Oh. Well, that's good to know, Cobalt."

My heart squeezed at the way he said my name, right where the arrow's pain had been. But it was gone now, thanks to him.

I recalled that Gaius introduced me at the opening ceremony. Of course he knew my name. However...

This omega was naked, and he was my mate, and I still didn't know *his* name. I wanted to ask, but I was rendered speechless by his presence. He was cute and small. He had a strong scent, too. I smelled it from across the room. He must've sweated a lot on the plane.

"You're a pretty big guy, huh?" he asked, his eyes raking up and down my body.

Warmth tingled under my skin. There was a keen

glimmer in his eyes, and I suspected there was something deeper than simple curiosity in the way he examined me.

"Yes," I said. "And you are very little."

He grinned wider, not offended by my observation in the slightest. "Sure am. You could probably fold me in half and stick me in your pocket, big boy."

I liked that idea. That way, we'd never be apart.

Impatience seized my blood. I couldn't stand not knowing his name for a second longer.

"Tell me your name," I said.

He bowed. "Muzo Zavala, at your service."

My dragon rumbled within me, pleased. He was at ease now, and I was, too.

There were no more barriers between us. Everything else faded into the background, unimportant. I only wanted to claim Muzo as my mate.

No longer burdened by ignorance, I took a step closer to him. Muzo tilted his head but didn't budge. As I approached, another whiff of his scent hit me. It came in layers—first, there was an unnatural, fake baby powder scent. But I wasn't interested in that. I wanted what was beneath it.

My dragon searched out Muzo's true scent. It shot straight through my system, making me shiver. He smelled of tangy sweat and omega musk. Closing my eyes, I leaned in to sniff deeper, to fill my lungs with his essence.

"Uh, whoa, hey, hey," Muzo said, sounding concerned.

I opened my eyes. "What is wrong?"

Then I recalled he was still naked, and I'd barged into his room uninvited moments earlier. He was my fated mate. I knew that to the core of my soul. But perhaps I was moving too fast for his comfort. Dragons were inherently selfish creatures. We wanted what we wanted, when we wanted it. But as an alpha, my need to protect my loved ones was even stronger. For him, I would wait.

Muzo wrinkled his nose. "Um, I smell *really* bad right now. I was actually gonna hop in the shower and scrub myself raw."

I had no idea what he was talking about. I stared at him, waiting for clarification.

When I didn't respond or move away, Muzo said, "Oh, no. I broke Cobalt."

"I'm not broken. What you said was absurd. You smell wonderful."

Now Muzo was confused. He sputtered, "What? Everyone I've talked to for the past, like, two weeks has told me how sweaty and nasty I am!"

"They are wrong," I stated. Plain and simple.

My dragon soul wouldn't accept distance between us any longer. I leaned in until Muzo was enveloped in my shadow, then brought my nose to the space where his arm met his chest. He made a high-pitched sound.

"Uh, what'cha doing there, Cobalt?" he asked, flustered.

"I am smelling you."

My nostrils flared as I took a deep breath of *him*. He smelled of sweat, yes, but also so much more. His pheromones bypassed my brain and activated my body's instinctive lust response. Rich masculine spiciness mixed with delicate floral notes. Below that was a layer of heady omega musk, thick as incense and just as intoxicating.

Without realizing it, I'd buried my nose in his armpit, sucking up as much of my fated mate's scent as possible. The temperature of his skin rapidly increased.

"Um," Muzo said, his voice cracking.

I didn't want to stop, but he clearly wanted my attention. "Hm?"

"You know better than me—being a dragon and all—but, uh, is breaking into a naked guy's room and smelling him... allowed on the Dragonfate Games?"

That was the last thing on my mind, but he did have a point. The camera crew and nosy hotel neighbors might still be outside his room. They didn't matter to me, but if they bothered Muzo, I'd scatter them like bugs.

Muzo raised an eyebrow. "By the way, are you pranking me right now, or are you actually super into my pit smell? It's fine either way, I just wanna know."

"I love it," I growled. "I wouldn't lie about that."

The color of Muzo's cheeks deepened and his brows shot up. "Oh, well, then..." He coughed softly. "Carry on, I guess? Like I said, I was about to shower—which is why I'm naked—but who am I to say no to the alpha dragon?"

I paused. Did he not *want* me to smell him?

A sudden worry struck me. I hoped my size didn't intimidate him. Frightening my fated mate by accident was my worst nightmare.

As painful as it was, I pulled away. "I'm sorry. I was insensitive. I won't obstruct you from showering."

Muzo watched me curiously, then snorted in amusement. "You're kinda weird. I like that in an alpha. I'm weird, too—though I gotta say, sniffing naked strangers is pretty out there, even by my standards." He cocked his head. "So, are you just gonna stand there like a sexy lawn ornament, or are you gonna come with me?"

"Come with you?" I echoed. I expected to be gently evicted from the room, not invited further in.

Muzo grinned. "Sure. Why not? You've already seen my bare butt and smelled my armpits and all. Doesn't get much more intimate than that, right?"

Mental images of various sensual acts flashed in my head.

"It could," I said honestly.

Muzo cackled with laughter. "You're funny. Anyone ever told you that?"

"No."

Waving me towards the bathroom, Muzo said, "C'mon, big boss. Let's get soapy."

SEVEN

Muzo

THINGS I DIDN'T EXPECT to happen today: the eldest alpha dragon ripping the door off my room, barging in unannounced, and seeing my entire naked ass.

Things that happened: *that.*

And now, because he stood there like a lost puppy I couldn't bear to kick out, I was leading him to the bathroom. What a day.

I didn't *want* to kick him out, though. Pretty much the opposite. He was so adorably clueless and weirdly innocent, like a caveman stepping into the modern world. If any other alpha had literally ripped my door off its hinges, I might've freaked out, but not with Cobalt. His presence was innately calming.

He reminded me of the ocean. I mean, he *was* blue all over. His hair was shades of cerulean—deeper blue with ripples of clear, sky blue. His blazer and trousers matched his hair, like he was forced to walk around in a color-coded outfit. Hell, maybe he was so the TV audience could instantly tell the dragons apart.

Oh, right. The audience. I'd forgotten about the whole TV show thing. Kinda hard not to when the biggest, sexiest man alive breaks into your room, scopes your booty, and excitedly sniffs your armpits.

I led Cobalt to the bathroom, which was almost the size of my old apartment. Pure white tiles sprawled out in every direction, sparkling with a spotless sheen. The shower was a box of glass with a fancy stainless steel showerhead.

"Here we are," I announced, gesturing to the space as if it were my own. "Though I bet you're familiar with it already, since it's your hotel and all."

Cobalt looked around nonchalantly. "I've never been inside before."

"Huh?"

His gaze settled back on me. "I only came here to find you."

Dammit, there it was again, those words that made my skin tingle. I didn't think he was even trying to be sweet. He was just genuinely wholesome.

"Oh," I said, surprised. "Why's that?"

Cobalt thought about it for a moment.

"I had to," he finally replied.

When he didn't elaborate, I shrugged. "Huh. Well, that's that."

Cobalt stared at me, waiting to follow my lead. Once again he reminded me of an overgrown puppy. I'd never had a puppy before—it's kinda weird to own a real animal when you're a shifter and all—so this was fun for me.

"Well, I dunno what you're gonna do, but *I'm* gonna take a shower," I told him. "I haven't had a proper one for —" I was about to say two weeks, but the mortifying ideal of confessing that to the sexy-caveman-puppy was too much to bear. "A while," I finished.

Cobalt had no comment. He didn't move at all except

for a slight furrow in his brow, like the fact that I was about to shower was disappointing to him.

What an adorable weirdo.

Since I was already undressed for the occasion, I stepped into the shower. Cobalt regarded me curiously. It was like a reverse horror movie. Instead of unexpectedly running into a man while naked in the shower, the man was already present.

"Here I go," I announced as I reached for the dial. I felt like I had to narrate everything I did to entertain Cobalt because I didn't want him to get bored and leave.

Just before I turned the water on, Cobalt approached the shower. His gaze drifted from the showerhead perched high on the tile wall down to me.

"It's difficult for you to reach," he pointed out. "Let me do it."

He didn't move immediately. Instead he stared down at me like a stoic statue. His comment sounded like a non-negotiable demand, but he still waited for my input.

"Uh, sure?" I said. He was right. It was pretty high up, and I was shorter than the average omega.

Cobalt grabbed the showerhead and pulled it out of the wall. A long stainless steel cord trailed behind the head like a snake.

I gasped. "Whoa! I didn't know it did that."

"Yes. Now I can wash you thoroughly."

That was a series of words I didn't expect to hear.

"Come again?" I asked.

"I will wash you," Cobalt replied like it was the most normal thing ever.

My temperature rose a few degrees as I gawked at him. Was he for real?

"I must make up for the poor accessibility design in this

bathroom," Cobalt murmured. "I wasn't aware you couldn't reach the showerhead or all its features."

I blinked. "I mean, it's not the end of the world, it's still *functional* as a shower."

"No," Cobalt said, sounding almost grumpy. "You deserve the best."

Tick. Tick. Oh look, there goes my steadily rising temperature again.

Seriously, what was with this guy? Five minutes ago he didn't even know my name, and now he was selflessly devoted to me? Did I get altitude sickness on the plane and lose my sense of reality?

Cobalt's deep, steady voice confirmed that this was very much real. "I'll turn on the water now," he said.

"Wait, wait," I interrupted. "You're still in the shower with me."

Another disappointed flicker crossed his face. "Do you want me to step outside?"

"No, it's not that." I gestured to his pristine outfit. "Your clothes are gonna get wet. Aren't dragons, like, obsessed with their clothes?"

Cobalt's thick dark brows creased together. "No." Then he seemed to remember something and his face relaxed. "You must be thinking of my younger brother, Crimson. You were a contestant on that season, too, yes?"

"Oh, right." Shameful heat flushed my cheeks. "My bad."

Ugh, what an embarrassing mistake. I hoped Cobalt didn't think I was a ditz, or worse, a total dickhead.

He reached for the dial and turned it on. Water shot out of the showerhead and onto the tiled floor. Cobalt put his hand in the spray, waiting for the perfect temperature.

"I don't care for clothes the way my brother does," Cobalt said. "He dressed me in this outfit, but it makes no difference to me whether it is ruined or not. They're only clothes. They are replaceable—this moment with you is not."

My heart skipped like a pebble thrown across a pond. Why was that the sweetest thing I'd ever heard in my life?

"Okay, but at least take your shoes off," I said, pointing to his leather loafers. "My mom would cuff me over the head if I ever wore shoes in the house."

He nodded, then removed his shoes. "Forgive me."

"You are forgiven," I said with a grin. "You could take the rest of the clothes off, too. Dunno if you know this, but that's usually what people do in the shower."

Cobalt paused, then said, "I have a confession to make."

"Yeah?"

"When I said Crimson dressed me, I meant it literally. I have no idea how to escape this elaborate outfit."

Oh, gods. He really *was* an adorable caveman.

I chuckled as I grasped the front of his blazer. "How 'bout we try it together? It's clothes, not rocket science. I'm sure it's not *that* complicated."

Cobalt nodded solemnly. "I believe in you."

"First, we gotta take this thing off. Like so..."

I wriggled the blazer around his arms—or tried to. Even under the clothes, I could tell they were thick and effortlessly muscular. The blazer fit him perfectly, but it was tight. Cobalt squirmed in the directions I moved it in, which helped. Eventually, I stripped the blazer free.

"Aha!" I cried triumphantly. "One down, more to go."

I thought we were halfway there—until I saw the monstrosity that was his white undershirt. I expected there to be buttons like a normal shirt, but there weren't. How did he even put it on?

"What the..." I frowned. "Did Crimson *glue* this thing on you?"

"There are strings at the back," Cobalt said.

He turned around and sure enough, there they were, criss-crossed and winding up his spine. Maybe clothing *was* a subsection of rocket science.

I fumbled with the bottom strings, undoing them as I worked my way up Cobalt's back, but a problem quickly became apparent. I wasn't tall enough to reach half of them.

"Could you, uh, kneel down?" I asked.

Without a word, Cobalt lowered himself to his knees. My heart fluttered. I hadn't expected him—a freaking alpha dragon—to obey so easily. Back in the human city, I couldn't even convince my superintendent that I didn't own a dog—but here, I'd brought an alpha to his knees with a simple suggestion.

"Thanks," I said, reaching for the upper strings.

As my hands moved, I became painfully aware of how *huge* Cobalt was. His back was as broad as a brick wall, solid and sturdy. Warmth radiated from his skin. He smelled good, too, like the cologne section of a department store.

Trying to be sneaky about it, I leaned in to sniff the bottom of his neck where the last tied-off strings remained. I shivered as the pleasant scent filled my nose. It made my skin tingle in a funny way.

My fingers struggled to undo the last knot. I was too engrossed in Cobalt to concentrate. The longer I was near him—seeing him, smelling him, feeling his warmth beneath the fabric, hearing his soft intake and exhale of breath—the more flustered I became. My fingers turned into sweaty, useless appendages that couldn't even untie two pieces of string.

"Okay, this is harder than I thought," I confessed.

Cobalt nodded, taking my word for it. He slowly stood back up. "Thank you for trying. I'll be fine with clothes on. Washing you is more important."

He awakened the showerhead again. Steam and the sound of rushing water filled the room. Cobalt looked intensely down at me, like this was the most important thing he'd ever done.

It suddenly occurred to me that I was *extremely* naked in front of this *very* attractive alpha. I blushed under the passion of his gaze.

"Are you ready? I'll begin now," Cobalt said.

I'd expected to wash myself, since I was fully capable of it and all, but I wasn't about to turn down his offer.

"Y-yeah, sure."

Cobalt brightened. A hint of a smile appeared on his face, and I nearly melted. If that's how cute his smile was, I'd offer to let him wash me more often.

I closed my eyes and ducked my head under the water's stream. A content sigh slipped out of me. How long had it been since I'd had a hot shower? Way too long. I'd forgotten how nice they were.

The relaxing warmth of the water lulled me into a tranquil state. I was so mellowed out that my body swayed and fell forward.

Right into Cobalt's chest.

I made a soft sound of surprise. I probably should've pulled away, but I didn't want to. He was the perfect pillow. Besides, he didn't say anything, so I figured it was fine.

I stilled as something touched my head. It was Cobalt running his fingers through my wet hair. My heart picked up speed despite the calming sensation.

Should I say something? Should I insist I can wash

myself, thank you very much, even though I was blissfully enjoying every second of this?

A cap popped open. A second later, cool liquid joined Cobalt's fingers. He worked the shampoo into my scalp in circular motions. Another sigh escaped my lips. I leaned more of my weight against Cobalt, letting him hold me up. I didn't care about pride or any of that stuff. After the crappy couple of weeks I'd been through, I just wanted to feel good—and Cobalt was damn good at that.

Once my hair was thoroughly lathered, Cobalt washed it away. I was grateful the greasy feeling was finally gone. But my hair wasn't the only thing that was dirty. My body needed a good scrubbing.

I opened my eyes, figuring I'd do that part myself, but Cobalt had already grabbed the body wash and poured it into his palm. His brows knitted in concentration as he rubbed his hand against my chest, creating a circle of white bubbles. The scent of lilac and vanilla overpowered my tangy sweat.

"Where did this... fake baby smell come from?" Cobalt grumbled.

I recalled the perfume Alaric spritzed me with earlier.

"Oh, that? It's some baby powder perfume thing," I explained. Sensing his distaste for it, I added, "Don't worry, it's not mine. Alaric put it on me 'cause he didn't want me to stink up the plane."

A shadow fell across Cobalt's face as he made a weird, deep sound. Was he *growling*?

"Your natural scent is superior in every way," he said in a low voice. "Do not put it on again."

I laughed at how serious he was about it. "You got it, boss."

Calmer now, he said, "Lift your arms."

I raised them, exposing the armpits he'd so happily

sniffed earlier. Cobalt hesitated for a split-second before squeezing more body wash into his hand and rubbing it into my pits.

I squeaked in surprise. "Hey, that tickles."

"Sorry. Should I stop?"

"No way. Just warning you that I squirm when I get tickled."

The tiniest hint of a smirk curled Cobalt's lip. Oh no. Did he have a tickling fetish? Was I about to get tickled to within an inch of my life?

And why was I strangely okay with that idea?

Cobalt didn't end up tickling me. Not on purpose, anyway. He continued gently scrubbing my armpits, working up a lather until soap bubbles took over the place. When that was done, he moved across my chest, soaping up everything from my collarbone to my navel. The lower his hands descended, the faster my heart raced. Did he even realize how close he was to my junk? Was that his secret plan all along?

I searched his face. There was no hungry, sex-crazed expression, just gentle compassion and a slightly furrowed brow of concentration. Honestly, I wouldn't have cared if he *was* secretly planning to peruse my cock, but knowing that wasn't the first thing on his mind made Cobalt even sweeter in my book.

"I can, uh, take it from here," I suggested before Cobalt went to town scrubbing my dick like a car wash.

Cobalt handed the bottle over to me. I hadn't noticed until now because I'd been in my own little relaxed world, but he was soaking wet. His drenched blue hair clung to his forehead, and his white shirt was plastered to his skin, leaving nothing to the imagination. His huge pecs stretched the soggy fabric, and his hard nipples threatened to poke through it.

Was that water trickling down the corner of my mouth, or was I drooling?

I wrenched my gaze away from Cobalt's chest and focused my frenzied thoughts on washing my nether regions. I was acutely aware of his eyes on me the whole time. Never had I been so thrilled by a stranger watching me soap up my butt.

Cobalt still held the showerhead, so when I was good and lathered, I said, "Okay, you can spray me now."

He obliged, dousing me in warm water. I sighed in relief as the last of the suds disappeared down the floor drain. It was so nice to be clean.

Before I could do anything, Cobalt turned off the water, grabbed a towel, and wrapped it around me. The rich dragons didn't skimp on the towels—they were huge, thick, and fluffy. The luxurious towel soaked up all the water like a cotton ball.

Cobalt observed me. The top of the towel sat high on my neck while the bottom trailed on the floor.

"You are quite small," Cobalt remarked.

I snorted in laughter. "And you are quite big."

"It makes me want to protect you even more."

My chest squeezed. "I didn't know you wanted to protect me in the first place."

Cobalt stared at me in silence, like he was trying to find the right words. Finally, he grunted like the cute caveman he was.

"I think you—" He stopped abruptly, then shook his head and tried again. "I liked the way your sweat smelled. A lot. I liked it a lot." Another pause. "I'm not saying you can't shower. You smell good either way. I simply prefer your natural scent."

I blushed. This dragon was full of surprises, wasn't he?

"Um. Thanks," I said, breaking into a dumb grin. "You smell pretty damn good yourself."

Cobalt's thick brows inched higher. "You think so?"

I nodded. "I dunno if you're wearing cologne or what, but keep it up."

"I'm not."

"So you just smell naturally amazing. Good to know."

Cobalt flashed a wisp of a smile that sent butterflies soaring towards my throat. I swallowed. Was he getting cuter by the second, or was it just me?

As the silence stretched, I wondered what to do. Should I invite him to stay? Was that weird, since he technically owned the hotel? Would he even want to stay here? It wasn't like there was much to do in the hotel room besides laze around in the king-sized bed, watch TV, and cuddle.

Actually, that sounded nice. Mmm, cuddling...

Wait, what?

Before I could even think about unravelling that train of thought, the unhinged door burst open.

"I cannot believe Jade sent me, a father and fashion icon, to deal with this," Crimson complained dramatically. In a casual motion, he placed the broken door back where he'd found it. "And what in the name of Holy Drake happened to this door?"

I pointed at my blue dragon companion. "Cobalt happened to it."

Crimson dusted off his pristine suit before looking at me in surprise. "Oh, Muzo, it's you. Good to see—" He fell silent, twisting his head towards his older brother. His ruby eyes narrowed as he glanced back and forth between us. "Interesting..."

"What are you doing here?" Cobalt asked.

The other alpha sighed. "Did my entrance speech not get the point across? I'm here to fetch you and attempt to undo this destruction you left in your wake." Crimson nodded at the busted door hinges.

Cobalt sulked like a toddler. "I don't want to leave."

"And I don't want to be an errand boy, but such is life." Crimson shrugged. "Come along, Cobalt. There will be plenty of time for you two to *play* later."

Before Cobalt could object, Crimson grabbed him by the arm and eased him out of the room like a rider coaxing a stubborn horse. I remembered from my time on season one that Crimson was a tall, handsome alpha—but next to him, Cobalt looked absolutely massive.

And he was way handsomer.

"Don't fret, you'll be reunited soon enough," Crimson reassured us with a smirk. "Don't forget the first challenge is tomorrow. Oh, and Muzo, I'm sending someone to fix this door ASAP, so don't complain to Omega Resources, all right? Ciao!"

The broken-yet-soon-to-be-fixed door shut behind them, and I was left alone with the butterflies in my tummy and the memory of Cobalt looking wistfully over his shoulder at me.

EIGHT

Cobalt

AS THE ELDEST BROTHER, I was usually the one who did the stern sit-downs and administered the gentle scoldings.

I wasn't used to being on the other end of it.

Once Crimson led me behind the hotel, he and Jade cornered me like a pair of disappointed teachers. Jade pushed up his glasses with a sigh, while Crimson crossed his arms.

"I've been told you disappeared after the opening ceremony, then proceeded to cause unnecessary property damage," Jade said mildly. "Care to explain what happened?"

Words were difficult in the first place. Describing what happened between me and Muzo was impossible.

I clutched my chest where the ache had been. "I had to find him," I murmured.

"Find who?"

"Muzo."

Jade shot a slightly confused look at Crimson, who nodded in confirmation.

"You broke down Muzo Zavala's door because you had to find him?" Jade repeated.

"Yes."

"Did anyone see you?"

Crimson interjected. "Only about two dozen people rubbernecking in the hallway, crew and contestants alike."

"Oh, dear." Jade gave Crimson a pointed look. "At least you and Thystle were stealthy about your forbidden encounters."

"Yes, an attempt was made," Crimson replied. "The same can't be said about Cobalt's door-demolishing ways. Those hinges were utterly annihilated."

All of this administrative drudgery was keeping me from Muzo. An impatient growl rolled in my throat.

"I don't care about the hinges," I said. "I care about Muzo. I would break his door in all over again."

"By the way, this has been bothering me," Crimson complained. He thrusted an accusatory finger towards me. "Why is the beautiful outfit I picked for you *soaking wet?* And where is your blazer? It's pure merino wool!"

"Oh." I pinched the wet shirt, which I'd forgotten about. "I was in the shower with Muzo. I must've left it in his room."

Crimson made a shrill, gutted sound. He looked like he was about to pass out.

"We'll get the blazer back," Jade promised.

"It's too late. It's ruined," Crimson muttered under his breath. "All my effort was wasted on this... this *lizard-brain!*"

Crimson must've been quite upset. He'd never insulted me before. It didn't bother me. Showering with Muzo was worth the life of an outfit.

"Now, let's all calm down," Jade said gently, putting a hand on Crimson's shoulder. "Why don't you go snuggle with Taylor until you relax?"

Crimson nodded shakily, then stalked off like the

world's most haggard man. When he was gone, Jade shook his head.

"He's dramatic, but it *is* his hoard, you know," Jade reminded me.

"I know," I murmured, feeling guilty.

If one of my brothers had treated my hoard that way, I would've been upset, too. But none of them knew what I hoarded. It was hypocritical of me. I'd never allowed my brothers into my hoard because I feared their mockery or some other negative reaction, and here I was disregarding Crimson's hoard. I'd have to apologize to him later.

Jade flashed a sympathetic smile. "I'm going to go out on a limb and assume you've found your fated mate."

Feeling erupted in my chest. Hearing it from someone else validated the already ironclad emotions within me.

Muzo. My fated mate.

Yes, that felt right.

Too overwhelmed to speak, I nodded.

Jade didn't look surprised. "That's wonderful, Cobalt. I'm genuinely happy for you." He gestured to the stage further back on the beach. "However, as you're aware, we have a show to run. Reality TV is fueled by conflict, and the whole will-they-won't-they drama."

I stared at him with a frown. Wherever this was going, I didn't like it.

"Simply put, it's not good TV if there's no suspense," Jade explained. "And if you're googly-eyed over Muzo before the first challenge even begins, the audience will pick up on it."

"Let them," I growled. "I won't fake my emotions for people I don't even know."

Jade's pencil-thin brows rose. I was surprised at the ferocity of my own words. I wasn't the type to get worked up over little things.

But Muzo was more important than that. Being asked to smother my feelings for him was like asking me to pretend he wasn't my fated mate.

Jade's soothing green eyes subdued my rising fury. "You don't have to do anything you don't want to," he said calmly. "All I'm asking is that you don't jump on Muzo the second you're being filmed."

My frown etched deeper.

"And at least *acknowledge* the other contestants," Jade continued. "They came all this way for a chance to be your mate."

My insides roiled at the thought. I didn't want any of them that way. I only wanted Muzo.

"Why can't the show be about our deepening connection instead?" I grumbled.

Jade laughed. "I'll take note of that for future seasons. But keep in mind, you'll have to play along if there are to *be* future seasons."

The gravity of his statement grounded me. He was right. I wasn't the only alpha dragon on this island. Besides Crimson and Thystle, my younger brothers hadn't found their mates yet. If the Dragonfate Games tanked in popularity and no more omegas applied to be contestants, they might lose their chance.

My protective instincts swam back to the surface of my consciousness. I had a duty to put aside my own selfish desires and help my family.

Jade tilted his head with a reassuring smile. "Muzo isn't going anywhere. You're still free to choose him as your mate."

That was true. Muzo wouldn't disappear if I adhered to Jade's suggestion. I knew the location of his hotel room, and even if he was moved to a different one with a functional door, his scent was burned into my memory. My dragon would hunt him down.

I nodded stiffly and mumbled, "Okay. Sorry for the trouble."

"It's all right, Cobalt. I'm glad to see you all incensed for your mate's sake," Jade said. "You'll see Muzo tomorrow during the first challenge. Can you bear to be apart from him tonight? We don't need *two* hotel break-ins in one day."

I glanced ruefully up at the building. After a taste of spending time with my mate, I craved more, but Jade had sneakily put his foot down. If I was a lizard-brain, then Jade was a snake. He was cool and slippery, and had a way of convincing you of anything without a scrap of disagreement.

"Okay," I said.

Jade nodded primly before picking up his phone. "Excellent. Now, if you'll excuse me, I've got to make some calls about that door..."

NINE

Muzo

I HATED GETTING sand in my nose.

Sneezing loudly for the third time, I groaned. "C'mon, not again..."

The first challenge was set on the beach, so we'd assumed our animal forms. I got bored of waiting for Gaius to arrive and start the whole shebang, so I dug around in the sand for fun—only for my nostrils to get bombarded with tiny sand particles.

Poppy whimpered in concern beside me, his ears flattening against his head. He'd been giving me that sad expression a lot lately.

"Um... maybe if you stopped hunting for crabs, you wouldn't get sand in your nose?" he suggested.

I pawed at my nose. "Yeah, but I'm bored."

Poppy glanced over his shoulder. His yellowish-white fur was puffed up along his neck from nerves. "Gaius and Cobalt should be here any moment," he assured. "So, um, maybe you can stop doing that and, er, pay attention?"

What was up with Poppy? He seemed more anxious than usual.

I lifted my head, opened my mouth to reply, then sneezed again. Sand flew everywhere.

A disgusted scoff came from my left.

"It's called covering your mouth. Ever heard of it?" Alaric snapped. He drew up a white kitty paw and cleaned the offending grains from his whiskers.

"My bad," I said, sniffling. "It's only sand."

"That makes it *so* much better..." Alaric curled his feathery tail around his body and scanned the beach. "There are fewer contestants here than last time, thank gods."

Poppy nodded gratefully, then looked at me. "That's good. Maybe one of us will have a better chance of, um... winning."

Alaric narrowed his odd-colored eyes. "Since when have you possessed the competitive spirit, wolf?"

Despite being five times bigger than Alaric, Poppy shrank under the house cat's gaze. He shuffled his paws together, staring down at the sand. "Um, I'm not really, I just—"

My nose erupted in a sudden sneeze. I swear the force of it was enough to knock me on my butt.

Alaric took two deliberate steps away from me. "Never mind," he muttered.

Poppy's shoulders slumped, as if relieved that the conversation was cut short. I was about to ask him what was up when gasps and murmurs filled the air. I turned around, following the crowd's shifting attention, then bolted upright when I noticed the arrival of two people— Gaius and Cobalt.

My eyes snapped instantly to Cobalt. How could I not stare at him? He was huge, tall and broad-shouldered, his blue hair striking even against the backdrop of the ocean. His rugged face was expressionless as he stood next to

Gaius, waiting for him to take the lead. Cobalt stood like an unmoving statue except for the slight knit of his brow and the tilt of his head as he scanned the crowd, searching for someone.

Was he looking for me? I held my breath as the thought crossed my mind.

And then Cobalt met my gaze.

My heart pounded like a drumbeat at two-times speed. He was just so cute. And cool. And handsome. And every other adjective I could think of.

"Muzo?" Poppy asked.

"Huh? What?"

"Your tail's wagging... a lot."

"I'm excited for the challenge," I said, which wasn't a lie.

Poppy said nothing, but he followed my line of sight. He crossed and uncrossed his paws. Did he want to say something?

If he did, there wasn't time. Gaius's charismatic voice boomed over the beach. "Welcome, omegas, to the first challenge of the third Dragonfate Games!"

The response was a chorus of excited cries. It struck me then how many people were here vying for Cobalt's love.

A weird, stringy feeling skittered unpleasantly in my belly. It caught me off guard. That had never happened before. In the previous two Games, I was happy just to be along for the ride. But now, when I imagined someone else beating me in the challenges, I didn't like it. Weird.

"Today's challenge is all about testing your water affinity," Gaius said. In his typical fashion, he wore a flamboyant Hawaiian shirt—this one was searing cyan blue with crisp white waves to match today's theme. He swept his arm towards the water, indicating a wide semi-circle of orange buoys.

"Not another swimming challenge," Poppy murmured, flattening his ears. "I only made it the first time because of Taylor's help..."

Alaric's whiskers twitched in annoyance. "Indeed. I thought we'd moved on from these absurd physicality-based challenges. I, for one, look forward to being tested on my impeccable intelligence."

For once, I didn't poke fun at Alaric. I was too busy staring at Cobalt. My eyes were drawn to him like a magnet. Was it my imagination, or did he get more hand-some the longer I looked at him?

"You can use your human or animal form, whichever you prefer," Gaius went on. "Isn't that right, Cobalt?"

Even hearing his name gave my heart goosebumps. I felt the fur rising on the back of my pelt.

Cobalt seemed distracted. He turned to Gaius like he'd forgotten he was there, nodded curtly, then locked eyes with me like it was his life's mission.

My tail wagged in the sand. I couldn't help it. Looking into his eyes—and seeing him looking back—just made me happy.

Gaius cut his hand through the air. "Go!"

Every shifter on the beach ran for the water—except me. I hung back. There were a lot of bigger animals present, like horses, deer, bears, and wolves. I didn't want to get trampled under their hooves and paws.

Besides, what was the big hurry? Gaius didn't say anything about a race. He only mentioned water affinity.

Alaric was already in the water, but Poppy skidded to a stop by the shoreline and shot me a confused glance.

"What are you doing, Muzo?" he asked. "Hurry!"

"I'm comin', I'm comin'," I said.

When the cartoonish cloud of sand settled, I trotted towards the ocean, but when my fur suddenly prickled, I paused.

Cobalt's gaze was on me. He was as still as a statue, but I recognized the tenderness in his expression. My tail swooped happily from side to side.

It felt like he was trying to tell me something, but what?

"Muzo!" Poppy cried.

Letting out a whimper of dismay, Poppy circled behind me, pressing his weight into my butt, and pushed me towards the water.

"Whoa, hey, I appreciate the boost, but I can do it myself, Pops," I said.

"You have to go faster," Poppy urged. "Look, all the other omegas are halfway through a lap, and you're not even in the water yet."

I wrinkled my nose. Everyone else was paddling hard, rushing in circles, but was that really what the challenge was about? Had they watched season one of the Games, when we'd done a similar race challenge for Crimson, and assumed this was the same?

My gut told me otherwise. Cobalt wasn't Crimson. He was his own alpha dragon, and the challenge reflected that.

"You go on ahead," I told Poppy. "I'll catch up."

Poppy looked torn. I could tell he wanted to stay and help me, like Taylor helped both of us, but he also wanted to believe my reassurance.

"Okay," he finally murmured. "But please try to do well, all right?"

What a weird thing to say. "'Course I will. Go on, ya big white furball, I'm right behind you."

Poppy frowned, then took off, doggy-paddling in circles like everyone else.

I stepped forward. The flowing tide caressed my two

front paws. It was a hot day, and the cool water felt nice.

I closed my eyes. The chaos of the beach and the challenge disappeared. For a moment, it was just me and the water.

As if awakened by the ocean's touch, an old memory suddenly came back to me. I inhaled. The smell of salt, the sun on my skin, and the cool breeze that danced along the water were brightly nostalgic.

But it wasn't nostalgia for the previous two Games. It was older than that. Something I'd all but forgotten about in the years since it happened.

A shiver ran along my pelt. With my eyes still shut, I treaded deeper into the water until the waves lapped against my chest. I didn't struggle against them. I let them support me. My weight dissolved into nothing as I floated in the ocean's arms.

Oh, yeah. This was definitely familiar...

As I bobbed along, I realized that this reminded me of another feeling, too. It was just like when I'd rested my weight against Cobalt in the shower. I'd handed over my trust to him, and he'd returned it. I imagined it was Cobalt's strong arms holding me afloat instead of the ocean waves. Or maybe they were one and the same.

I was so relaxed I might as well have been in another world. I didn't hear the voices, or the splashing, or notice the incoming horde of shifters—or that I was directly in their path.

A second later, my body pitched underwater.

The calm spell was shattered. My eyes snapped open and my legs flailed as I spun out of control, caught in the undertow of all the racing animals. I tried to reach the surface, but there were too many bodies in the way.

The more I struggled, the less air remained in my lungs.

So I stopped.

The havoc of splashing bodies rushed overhead, blocking the sun. It was dark anyway, so I closed my eyes. Waiting.

Trusting the water.

And then, my trust paid off.

Out of nowhere, a powerful force grabbed me. My head breached the surface a second later. I gasped and sucked fresh air into my sore lungs until I could breathe normally again.

"Muzo."

The deep, gravelly voice sounded like a plea.

Cobalt's arms wrapped around my small canine body, pressing me against his wide, muscular chest. He held me with such gentle vehemence. It seemed like he'd never let me go.

"I've got you," Cobalt said, soft yet firm. A promise meant only for my ears. "Are you all right?"

"Yeah. I think so," I said breathily.

Cobalt let out a long, relieved exhale through his nose. "Good."

Still carrying me in his arms, he trudged towards the shore. For such a big man, his strides met little resistance. He cut through the water like a knife in butter.

When Cobalt reached the sand, Poppy rushed towards us. He'd reverted to human form and was wrapped up in a towel like the rest of the contestants. Gaius must've cut the challenge short when I nearly drowned and summoned the other omegas back to the beach.

"Muzo!" Poppy cried. "Oh, gods, I'm sorry, I should've stayed with you. I just looked back and suddenly you disappeared, and..." He put his hand over his mouth as he got choked up.

My heart squeezed in sympathy. I hated knowing I'd

upset Poppy, even by accident.

"Hey, Poppy, it's okay," I said. "Look, I'm fine! Cobalt saved me."

Poppy sniffled, gazing up at Cobalt with liquid brown eyes. "Thank you so much. I-I don't know what would've happened if you didn't intervene..."

"I will always protect Muzo," Cobalt promised. Since I was pressed to his chest, I felt the thick vibration of his voice as he spoke.

I noticed the adrenaline had already dissipated from my system. Now I only felt calm and safe. I could've cuddled into Cobalt's chest forever.

"Come," Cobalt said. "I'll take you to the medic."

"No, no, I'm fine, I swear," I protested. Then I shifted into human form and said, "Look, I've got all ten fingers and ten toes."

In the middle of all the hectic events, I'd forgotten that shifting made me naked.

Gaius sighed as he jogged closer to us. "Gonna have to censor that in post-production... Here, Muzo, take a towel." He grabbed one from a nearby crew member and tossed it at me.

Before I could catch it, Cobalt snatched it in mid-air, then draped it over my body like a baby blanket. A tiny smile formed in the corner of his mouth.

That sly dragon. Did he *like* that I was naked in his arms for the second day in a row?

Gaius resumed his hosting role. "Wow, talk about eventful! Rest assured that Muzo is safe after that incident."

I gave the closest cameraman a thumbs up.

"Well, Cobalt?" Gaius asked, facing him. "Should we try the challenge again tomorrow, or—"

"No," Cobalt stated. "I've already chosen a winner."

His fingers curled tighter into my body in a subtly possessive gesture. It sent electric jolts skittering across my skin.

As the silence lingered, my heart beat wildly in anxious anticipation. I'd missed half of the challenge and ended up half-drowned. There was no way Cobalt would announce *me* as the winner, would he?

Cobalt took a deep breath. I rose and fell with the great movement of his chest.

"It's Muzo," Cobalt finally said.

I tried not to wince at the shocked gasps and derisive snorts that came from the other contestants.

"He barely did anything," a nearby omega complained.

Another chimed in. "Yeah, he didn't join the race at all!"

Surprisingly, it was Alaric who leapt to my defense.

"I see," he said, crossing his arms thoughtfully. "The jackal had the right idea after all. Nowhere in Gaius's instructions did he mention a race. What he *actually* said was that the challenge tested our water affinity."

"That's right," Cobalt said, summoning everyone's attention. "Muzo was the only omega who *listened* to the water."

The other contestants exchanged bewildered glances. Meanwhile, Poppy and Alaric looked confused but pleased at my win. I noticed Poppy's shoulders sagging in relief, a stark contrast to how anxious he looked before the challenge started.

Gaius flashed a dazzling grin at the camera. "There you have it, folks, straight from the alpha dragon's mouth. The winner of the first challenge is Muzo Zavala! I hope you're looking forward to the prize—a date with Cobalt himself!"

TEN

Cobalt
___

THE OCEAN WOULD NOT HAVE LET Muzo drown. I knew that instinctively.

But the ocean didn't control people's behavior. They were the dangerous factor.

When Muzo disappeared under the mass of hooves and paws, I nearly lost control of my dragon. It took every scrap of willpower to keep him under control—because if it was up to him, he wouldn't hesitate to crunch every other omega between his fangs to get to Muzo.

But my human form wasn't slow, either. Not when it came to the water. I'd bolted to the shore, dove in, and swam towards Muzo's sinking body in the blink of an eye. The relief I felt when I hauled him to the surface and heard him take a breath was indescribable.

There was no way I'd lose him. Not when he was finally in my grasp.

After I'd chosen Muzo as the winner and the other contestants dispersed, Gaius sidled up to us. I was busy drying off Muzo's naked body with the towel. A crew member on standby held his clothes for him, but they'd been waiting for a while. I wouldn't be satisfied until I'd dried every inch of Muzo's skin.

"You know, there's been a lot of full-frontal nudity for a program that's supposed to be rated PG-13," Gaius remarked, nodding at the lurking camera crew.

I glared in their direction. Not everything had to be filmed. They scurried off when I uttered a low growl.

"That's not very nice, Mr. Big Scary Dragon," Gaius said. "That's what you're paying them to do, remember?"

I ground my teeth, biting back a hostile reply. My earlier conversation with Jade kept me in line. I had no choice but to put up with the presence of cameras and other contestants until the Games were over.

But it wasn't all bad. Muzo was safe, and thanks to my thorough towelling, he was dry. When he met my eyes, he smiled so brightly, it lit up his whole face.

That made everything worth it.

"I'VE GIVEN up being your personal stylist," Crimson said with a huff. "If you want fashion advice, go to Thystle. But heed my warning—you'll look like you walked straight out of a My Chemical Romance concert."

Thystle shot him a withering glare. "And what exactly is wrong with that?"

"Nothing, if you love eyeliner and the color black."

Thystle scowled. "Gerard Way is a queer icon, you arrogant, stuck-up lizard-brain. And in case you forgot, Matteo wears eyeliner and wears black when he performs, so I'd watch it if I were you."

I sat restlessly in my seat as I listened to my younger brothers argue. Jade had tasked them with preparing me for my evening dinner date, since they were both experienced with it, but the discussion had rapidly devolved into my fashion sense—or lack thereof.

Crimson huffed, holding up a hand. "All right, fine, I won't deny either of those things. My point is, Cobalt ruins every outfit I put him in. First it was the wool blazer, and then it was the pure cotton shirt logged with salt water."

"The shirt dried in the sun," I pointed out, nodding at it draped on the back of the chair.

"So did the salt," Crimson said tartly.

Thystle rolled his eyes. "Ignore Crimson. You're not trying to impress random people with your clothes. Just your date."

"His name is Muzo," I said.

Thystle grinned. "I know. I've met him before." He tilted his head, giving me a curious look. "He's cute. Not my type, obviously. But you're pretty smitten with him, aren't you?"

My fingers clenched on my knees. "He's my fated mate," I said under my breath.

Crimson paused filing through my meagre closet and blinked. After a moment, he sighed. "Then what are we wasting time for? Here, put these on."

He grabbed a navy-blue shirt and black pair of trousers, then plopped them in my lap. It was a simple outfit, but I liked it that way.

I stood up from my seat. From my full height, Crimson and Thystle looked smaller. But nobody was as small as Muzo. He could practically fit in my pants pocket. Thinking about that made me smile.

I wasn't used to this feeling. As the oldest, I was supposed to be the most experienced in all things, yet when it came to fated mates, it was brand-new to me. The instincts were there, but not the knowledge.

Crimson and Thystle were both dedicated partners and

loving fathers. Perhaps it was time for me to ask *them* for advice.

"What did you do," I began slowly, "when you knew?"

A knowing grin spread over Crimson's face. "Oh, Cobalt, you're really in it now. Let me guess—you want to storm over to the beach, scoop up Muzo in your arms, then fly away into the sunset, leaving the Dragonfate Games and all its associated nonsense behind."

"Yes," I replied.

Crimson went on in a melodramatic tone. "And yet here comes Jade the Relentless, forcing you to stay the course. He insists on lying low, keeping your feelings a secret until the end of the Games, but how *can* you? You're in love!"

I nodded. "That's right."

"It's not that complicated," Thystle said casually. "Just find him after filming hours if you need to, uh... sate your urges. That's what I did with Matteo."

"And I did with Taylor," Crimson agreed.

I frowned in contemplation. Was it that simple? Perhaps I'd overthought it.

"Okay," I said. "Thanks."

Thystle tilted his head. "Is something bothering you, Cobalt?"

I stared at the floor. "Jade asked me to hide my feelings, but it's hard. I already know who my fated mate is. I don't want to pretend to be interested in the other omegas."

"We know. The same thing happened to us," Thystle agreed. "You don't have to pretend to be attracted to them."

That made me feel slightly better.

"I don't want to ruin the show and destroy the opportunity for the rest of our family," I murmured.

Sympathy flashed across Thystle's face. "Oh, Cobalt. You're not gonna ruin anything."

Crimson stroked his chin. "Hang on. You said *you* know who your fated mate is. The question is, does *he* know?"

I paused. That never crossed my mind.

"How would he *not* know?" Thystle shot back, raising a brow. "Cobalt broke into his fucking room the day he arrived. He'd have to be dense not to—"

As Thystle cut himself short, he stared deadpan at Crimson.

"And there, my brothers, is our answer," Crimson replied with a grin. "This is Muzo Zavala we're talking about, not Albert Einstein."

"Muzo isn't stupid," I growled. "He just thinks differently."

There was no malice in Crimson's tone. "Kind of like you?" he offered.

The mild flare of anger settled down. He didn't mean anything negative by that statement. I was just feeling over-protective of my mate.

And incredibly pent-up. But I didn't want to mention that to my brothers.

"My point is, Muzo might not realize how you feel," Crimson explained. "So, use your time on the Games to convince him."

That made sense. Muzo was unassuming and went with the flow. My actions so far might not have meant anything to him. I had to prove how I felt with conviction, with no room for misunderstanding.

"All right. I'm ready for my date," I announced.

ELEVEN

Muzo

I WAS SO NOT ready for my date.

After returning to my hotel room—which had a brand-new door on it—I discovered a luscious gift basket on my freshly made bed.

"Ooh," I said excitedly. Nobody had ever given me a gift basket before.

I picked up the accompanying handwritten card. I knew without checking the name signed at the bottom that it wasn't written by Cobalt—which was odd, since I'd never actually seen Cobalt's handwriting before. The letters were uniform and elegant, like it was printed from a computer instead of in pen.

> *Dear Muzo,*
> *Please accept our humblest apologies for the continued inconveniences you've experienced on this season of the Dragonfate Games. We hope this gift basket portrays the depths of our regrets, and our immense gratitude for your continued presence on the program.*
> *Sincerely,*
> *Jade Chromatimaeus*

I noticed there was more handwriting on the back of the card. When I flipped it over, my heart skipped a beat. The words were bigger, darker, and a bit disorderly, like each letter was painstakingly carved into the paper. I had a good idea of who wrote it before I got to the end.

MUZO,
SORRY ABOUT THE DOOR, AND THE NAKEDNESS.
TWICE.
I PICKED THE ITEMS IN THE BASKET. HOPE YOU
LIKE THEM.
I CANNOT WAIT TO SEE YOU TONIGHT.
COBALT

An eager laugh burst out of me. Even Cobalt's hand-written letters were adorable.

Wait a second.

Did he say he couldn't wait to see me? And that *he'd* made this gift basket for me?

My already-skipping heart barrelled into overdrive. I'd been secretly stoked to see him, but I didn't know he felt the same way.

Suddenly overwhelmed, I flopped on the bed. I'd won the first challenge, even though I didn't think my affinity for water was *that* strong. I wasn't an aquatic shifter—hell, I'd almost drowned.

Still, that wasn't the first time in my life the water had held me safely in its arms...

I pushed the irrelevant memory aside. A little nagging doubt in my mind wondered if Cobalt had picked me as the winner as a kind of apology, and the gift basket was just the cherry on top of it. The dragons always went above and beyond in their hospitality. It made me dread going back to the real world and dealing with my not-so-extravagant life.

I glanced at the basket. Curiosity got the best of me and I dug into it, dumping its contents on the bed.

"Whoa," I breathed.

There was so much to look at, I didn't know where to begin. High-quality chocolates, assorted gift cards in $100 increments, pure beeswax candles, luxury brand coffee beans, fancy lip balm, a bottle of aged red wine, expensive-looking lotion from a brand I'd never heard of... It was overwhelming.

But the best thing of all was a huge handmade dragon plushie in the same shade of blue as Cobalt's hair.

I reeled. Everything must've cost a fortune. I couldn't leave any of these generous offerings behind. But how was I going to make room for it all? My suitcase was already full of clothes, so that only left my meagre backpack.

And more importantly, where the hell was I gonna put it when I went back to the city? It wasn't like I had a home anymore.

My rush of excitement was dampened by reality. I bit my lip, feeling guilty. I didn't want to reject Cobalt's kind offering, but I didn't want all the expensive items to go to waste in a back alley somewhere.

No way. These were Cobalt's gifts. I was determined to make it work. The gift cards and lip balm were easy enough to stash in my pocket. I'd light the candles, slather the lotion on myself, and eat the chocolate during the trip. I was feeling peckish anyway. I'd snag a bite before the date.

What about the wine, coffee, and plushie?

Especially the plushie. I gazed into his little embroidered eyes. I couldn't abandon that face.

I could always leave behind some clothes to make

everything fit. After all, who needs pants when you have a giant blue dragon plushie?

I WAS INSTRUCTED to meet Cobalt on the beach at twilight. After snacking on expensive chocolate, I'd put on my best outfit for the date—which wasn't saying much because it was the only T-shirt and pair of jeans I had without holes in them—and left the hotel.

When I reached the shore, I noticed a lone figure by the water, as well as the lurking camera crew. They were on standby to record our date.

Right. Not only was this my first date ever in the history of my existence, but it would all be caught on film and broadcasted to a huge audience.

No pressure.

Cobalt stood facing the ocean. Behind him, the sky was a living watercolor painted in beautiful strokes of pink, orange, and violet. The water reflected the gorgeous colors as it ebbed and flowed at Cobalt's feet.

The sight of him gave me pause. Even from a distance, he was so *big*. It wasn't just his physicality, either. My shifter side sensed the behemoth dragon lurking within him. I'd seen it once for a brief moment during the first closing ceremony, and I hadn't forgotten it since. Cobalt's massive dragon form made the rest of his brothers look like skittering wall geckos.

As if sensing me, Cobalt suddenly turned around. His stoic face lit up, his smile softening his ruggedly handsome expression.

My chest squeezed. He'd mentioned looking forward to our date, but man, he seemed genuinely happy to see me.

I grinned in return and waved. Then I realized with a

mounting sense of awkwardness that I didn't know what to do. Should I wait for him to approach me, or should I meet him where he stood? What was the right thing to do on a date?

In the span of time that I uselessly deliberated, Cobalt had already reached my side. I craned my neck back to meet his gaze.

"Hi," I said in an unintended squeak.

"Good evening." Cobalt kept smiling. "I'm glad you made it."

"Course I did. The only thing that would've kept me away was if I fell in the toilet or something."

Cobalt's thick brows rose. "Are the toilets in the hotel too big for you? Just say the word and I'll arrange for a smaller one," he said seriously.

I chuckled. "No, no, I was joking. Thanks, though."

Cobalt relaxed, then offered his huge hand. "All right. Are you ready for dinner?"

Oh.

Oh, no.

Cold dread broke out across my skin. How could I forget something so important? In the previous two Dragonfate Games, the prize for winning the first challenge was a date—a *dinner* date.

And I'd just eaten two and a half bars of luxury chocolate.

"Um," I said.

Cobalt regarded me closely. He seemed concerned that I hadn't taken his hand yet. "What's wrong?"

"I, uh... I'm not hungry," I admitted in a small voice. "You know the gift basket you sent me?"

Cobalt perked up, his blue eyes shining. "Yes. Did you like it?"

"Yeah, I loved it," I blurted. "The problem is, I loved it

a little too much. I, um... I ate a ton of chocolate before our date. Because I forgot dinner was involved. I'm *so* sorry."

I felt like a dumb kid who'd ruined his appetite by stealing from the cookie jar right before his mom cooked his favorite food. Swamped with guilt and regret, I hung my head, waiting for his admonishment.

Cobalt's finger tipped my chin up. I blinked at him in confusion.

"I don't care about that," he said plainly. "I'm glad you enjoyed the chocolate. I put it there just for you."

Warmth seeped into my cheeks.

"But what about dinner?" I asked.

"We'll postpone it. We can have dinner at any time," Cobalt said.

"But... this was the prize for winning the challenge," I reminded him.

"Then we will make it the prize for a different challenge."

"What if I don't win any other challenges?" I asked.

A shadow flashed across Cobalt's eyes. His scornful brows knitted together, like that wasn't even close to the realm of possibility.

"Never mind that," Cobalt rumbled. "Let's take a walk instead."

Hope fluttered in my chest. I'd totally botched dinner, but Cobalt still wanted to spend time with me on a date.

"That sounds awesome," I said.

Cobalt's smile made me melt. It was so tender, you'd think we'd known each other our whole lives.

I followed him as he strolled to the shoreline. The sound of crying gulls and lapping ocean waves relaxed me. At first, I took two steps for every one of Cobalt's paces, but then he noticed I had trouble keeping up with his long strides and he slowed down to my speed.

"You smell different," Cobalt said suddenly. He didn't mask his disappointment.

"I do?"

Cobalt stopped and leaned in, scenting the air around me. I blushed. As a canine shifter, I wasn't averse to being sniffed, but it felt unusually intimate when Cobalt did it. Not that I minded, though.

"It smells like roses," Cobalt said, as if that was a bad thing.

"Oh! It's because of that lotion. The one you put in the gift basket."

Cobalt grunted, apparently reassured it was temporary. "I forgot about that." He paused for a beat. "I should've put unscented lotion in the basket instead."

My blush deepened as I recalled the shower incident. I couldn't think about it without my temperature rising.

"Because you like my natural scent, right?" I offered.

"Yes," Cobalt said, his deep voice almost a growl. Flurries of feeling swirled in my chest.

I smiled up at him. "That was really nice of you, by the way. The whole gift basket thing. No one's ever given me one before." I bit my lip. "Actually, while I'm blabbing about stuff that's never happened to me, can I confess something else?"

Cobalt nodded. "You can tell me anything, Muzo."

My heart rate picked up speed. The way he looked at me and said my name and said such nice things unleashed a swarm of butterflies in my chest. Their wings tickled the inside of my ribs, making me feel warm and itchy. The sensation was so powerful I forgot how to talk for a few seconds—and believe me, *that* was a feat.

"So... I've never actually been on a date before," I told him.

The blue depths of Cobalt's eyes flashed again. He inched closer, his massive presence engulfing mine like a protective bubble.

"What's wrong with that?" he asked. The question was honest, not defensive.

I shuffled my feet in the sand. "Nothing, technically, I guess? But I'm inexperienced at dating. I have no clue what I'm doing right now."

The corners of Cobalt's mouth lifted into a soft smile. "Then we'll be inexperienced together."

Was I imagining the hint of relief in his voice? And if not, why would Cobalt care if I'd been on dates before? We weren't actually dating, so it wasn't like he could be jealous, right? Maybe it was his competitive dragon's pride, and he wanted to do a better job than my non-existent exes.

I grinned. "Hey, if it means anything, this is the best date I've ever been on."

Cobalt regarded me for a long beat, like he could've looked at me forever. I wasn't immune to him, either. I was sucked into the depths of his blue eyes, spellbound to the point that I forgot to breathe.

As I sucked in a rush of air, I noted Cobalt's scent along with it. The thick, spicy musk he exuded was irresistible. A peculiar tingle of warmth shimmied down my spine and pooled between my thighs.

I'd never been on a date. I'd never been in love. I'd never even kissed anyone.

But right now, I *really* wanted to kiss Cobalt.

I always found it weird how they did it in movies—closing your eyes and leaning in and all that. What if the other person didn't meet you halfway?

Looking at Cobalt, though, I had no doubts. He saved me from drowning, and he promised Poppy he would protect me.

He'd be there.

With my heart racing out of control, I slowly closed my eyes and pushed up on the balls of my feet, stretching as high as I'd go. For me, it was a long way up; for Cobalt, a long way down.

I heard my blood beating in my ears. I had no idea what was about to happen, but I didn't dare open my eyes.

Then I felt the movement of air ghosting over my face. Following the motion came a whiff of strong alpha—Cobalt's scent. My heart beat so fast I worried it might explode.

Cobalt was there. He was *right* there.

He was gonna kiss me.

Suddenly, the tide roared onto the shore. Cold water doused me from the waist down. I yelped in astonishment, leaping up instinctively to avoid the cold.

This caused two things to happen.

One, I accidentally jumped right into Cobalt's waiting arms.

Two, I accidentally crushed our mouths together.

I mean, yeah, I was *trying* to kiss him in the first place, but this was no beautiful movie kiss. This was two faces colliding in an awkward, unsexy way. Teeth and bruised lips were involved. It was a kissing massacre.

"Ack!" I blurted. "I'm sorry, that isn't what I was trying to do."

Cobalt's mouth hung open. The spray from the tide splashed his hair. Loose strands of it fell across his forehead, ruining his otherwise well-put-together vibe. He looked adorably silly.

And then he started laughing. A deep, honest belly laugh belted from his lips.

I'd seen him smile, but never heard him laugh. The effect was instantaneous. It slammed me deep in my core. I *loved* that sound.

Cobalt's happiness was infectious. I burst out laughing, too. The two of us lost it until we ran out of air.

When I'd caught my breath, I said, "Sorry I ruined our first kiss. And my first kiss *ever*."

"That was your first?" he asked.

"Uh huh. Told you I'm not experienced."

His smile twisted into an unexpectedly mischievous smirk. "Good. We'll do it over and over until we get it right."

My stomach flipped. Did he *want* to kiss me over and over?

Aside from the kissing debacle, I couldn't help but think this *was* a little romantic. Cobalt hadn't set me down, so I was curled up in his strong alpha arms like a damsel in distress against a picturesque backdrop of sky and ocean.

Cobalt pressed his forehead to mine. I shivered at the damp feeling of his hair brushing against my warm skin.

"Tonight. Your room. Kissing practice," Cobalt said quietly.

My brain short circuited. I gawked, certain I'd misheard him.

"What do you think, Muzo?" he asked.

My toes curled at the sultry way he murmured my name.

"Yup. Yes," I said, nodding for good measure. "Good idea."

Satisfaction glittered in Cobalt's sapphire eyes.

"Then I'll see you later," he promised.

TWELVE

Cobalt

I DIDN'T BREAK the door this time.

Taking my brothers' advice, I waited until after hours to breach the hotel. I entertained the idea of flying to Muzo's balcony in my dragon form, but it was too gigantic to be stealthy. Going on foot in human form was less of a headache.

I stalked past the front desk and beelined for Muzo's room. My late-night visit wasn't technically allowed, but I didn't care. The film crew was off work for the day, so nobody should be there to record my infraction. Besides, this hotel was my property. The whole island was mine.

And now, Muzo was about to be mine, too.

I didn't check the room numbers. I'd already memorized which one belonged to him. When I arrived in front of it, I noticed the new door, and was struck by the urge to rip *this* one off its hinges, too.

Instead, I gave a single stiff knock.

Muzo swung it open immediately, like he'd been waiting for my arrival. His face lit up the second he laid eyes on me.

"Hi, Cobalt," he said through a smile.

The sight of him after a brief time apart reignited the heat between my thighs. I didn't waste a second longer. I stepped into the room, letting the door shut behind me. This time, there were no prying onlookers lurking in the hallway. We had this moment to ourselves.

"I missed you," I said.

Muzo's cheeks flushed as he laughed. "Really? It's only been, like, two hours."

"Any time apart is too long."

He ducked his head, the blush turning a shade darker. "I missed you, too. I kept thinking about our date. I had so much fun. And the kiss was..." He swallowed visibly. "Nice."

I swept closer to him. No more time or distance stood between us.

"I'm here," I assured him, taking his hands in mine.

The size difference shocked me. They were so small and soft, only half as big as mine. Powerful protective feelings surged to the surface of my being. It was similar to how I felt about my blood family, but innately different. This was deep and potently romantic. I'd never felt this way about any omega before.

"So, uh, your hands are pretty big," Muzo began, glancing at them before mischievously meeting my gaze. "Does the rest of you match?"

"If you're asking if I have a large cock, the answer is yes."

Muzo broke out into a breathy laugh. "Hey, I was tryin' to be subtle about it." Looking over his shoulder at the king-sized bed, he added, "Speaking of being subtle, I dunno if you got the hint, but I'm inexperienced at the whole spectrum of romance. If you catch my drift."

My brows furrowed. "I do not."

Muzo's cheeks gradually turned a deeper color. "Right.

Okay. I'm..." He lowered his voice to a barely discernible mumble. "A virgin."

Why was he so shy about it? That meant nothing to me.

I lifted his hand and pressed a kiss to the back. "Then I will take you as slowly as you need," I promised.

Muzo's eyes widened, their dark depths glinting with a storm of feeling. He licked his lips before letting out a weak laugh. "You really know how to fluster a guy, Cobalt. C'mon, let's at least sit on the bed. I'm getting weak in the knees here."

I followed him to the king mattress. There was plenty of space for both of us, even though I took up the majority of it. I noticed the blue dragon plushie sitting squarely on top of the pillows at the base of the headboard.

"Do you like that?" I asked, nodding to it. "I asked Taylor to sew it."

Muzo gasped, gathering the plushie into his arms. "Do I *like* it? I'm obsessed with him! If I only got to bring one thing back home with me, it'd be this guy, no matter how many clothes I had to—" He stopped suddenly, his mouth hanging open, then he grabbed a half-eaten chocolate bar off the bedside table. "Hey, you wanna share this? If I eat any more by myself, I might explode."

I didn't know why he changed the subject so suddenly, but I figured it was hyperactivity caused by all the sugar. I leaned forward to take a bite.

"Mm," I said. "Not bad."

"Not bad?" Muzo echoed in disbelief. "This is probably the best stuff money can buy. And you bought it for me."

"Of course I did. I'd buy you anything you ever wanted."

I took another small bite while Muzo blushed.

"I'm not a big chocolate fan," I admitted. "But it tastes sweeter since you brushed it with your lips."

Muzo fanned himself. "Haha. Did they crank up the heat in here, or is it just me?"

He seemed nervous. If this was his first time engaging in any romantic act, I understood why. As much as I wanted to jump right into it, Muzo's needs came first. My dragon and his mating instincts had to be patient.

"I brought something," I said.

"Another gift? Cobalt, seriously, you've given me enough."

"Not quite." I pulled out a small bottle of unscented baby oil from my back pocket. "I thought you might enjoy a massage after your chaotic day."

"Y-you're gonna massage me?" he asked, eyes going wide. "But that's so..."

"What?"

Muzo swallowed again. "Intimate."

His confusion baffled me—until I remembered what Crimson said earlier. Maybe it was his lack of romantic experience, but Muzo didn't realize I was interested in him that way, despite what I thought were over-the-top attempts at getting the point across. If gift baskets and saving his life and offering to give him a private massage didn't make it clear enough, I had no choice but to be blunt with him.

"Muzo," I said.

He tilted his head, his fluffy hair flopping to the side. "Yeah?"

"I am romantically and sexually drawn to you."

A sputtering sound escaped Muzo's lips. "What?" he squeaked, his cheeks alight.

I leaned forward so he could witness the resolve in my

eyes. "I *want* you," I said, my voice halfway to a growl. "Only you."

Muzo stared at me like his brain had broken. "But I'm —and *you're*—hoo boy, this makes no sense."

I inched closer. "Kiss me again, then tell me it makes no sense."

A soft expression came over Muzo's face. The mask of constant humor slipped away, revealing a hesitant tenderness beneath.

Taking a shaky breath, he angled his head. His lashes fluttered shut as he crept closer.

My heart squeezed with affection, and I closed the gap. Our lips met in a satin kiss. The soft feeling of Muzo's mouth and his up-close scent drove me wild. The sensation rocketed down my spine to the base of my cock. A simple, chaste kiss with my fated mate was enough to make me instantly hard.

Muzo didn't pull away. He stayed, exploring. He parted his lips and poked out his tongue, tentatively dragging it across my lower lip. When I moaned quietly, he stiffened, then did it again. Was it turning him on, too?

My tongue darted out and caressed his, making Muzo whimper with need. He threw his hesitation out the window and kissed back twice as hard. I was happy to let him earn confidence.

When he pulled away, his eyes were bright and his cheeks were flushed. His hesitant aura was gone. He gripped the covers tightly, staring at me, impatient for more.

"Well," he said breathlessly, a grin curving his mouth. "I still think this makes no sense. But I like it."

I smiled back. "Take your shirt off. I'll massage you."

Muzo shimmied out of his T-shirt and threw it aside. I scanned his body. I'd seen him naked before—twice—but there was a different kind of intimacy as he stripped. The previous times were accidents. Now, he was willingly offering himself to me. That heated my blood, made it rage through my veins. My pants grew tighter by the second.

My gaze drifted to Muzo's lower half. A slight bulge formed between his thighs. The sight of it made my blood burn even hotter.

"Turn around," I instructed.

Muzo settled on his knees in front of me. The top of his head came up to my mid-chest, so I had to angle myself accordingly. I popped the cap off the baby oil, poured a dollop in my palm, rubbed my hands together to warm it, then placed them on Muzo's back. He sighed contentedly as I worked my thumbs into his shoulders.

"Feels nice," he murmured.

He leaned back into my touch. His body was as light as a feather, and just as soft. Rubbing his supple skin made my cock harder, but I kept it in check. This evening was all about my mate's needs, not mine.

Still, I relished this opportunity. Getting to touch him and smell him was incredibly gratifying. I didn't realize how desperately I needed this alone time, this chance to worship him with my hands. After all Muzo had been through today, he needed this. He *deserved* this.

"Cobalt, you're growling," Muzo pointed out questioningly.

I halted and cleared my throat. "Sorry. I didn't notice."

"Everything okay?"

"Yes. It's a good growl."

Muzo chuckled. "I didn't know dragons had good or bad growls. Normally when canines growl, it ain't 'cause we're happy."

I leaned down so my cheek was against his temple. "Then it's time for you to learn about dragons."

He shuddered with a slight intake of breath. When I glanced down, I saw that the bulge in his pants had grown. His erection was hard and tenting now.

"Are you enjoying yourself?" I asked.

I already knew the answer. I wanted to hear him say it, to luxuriate in his own pleasure.

Muzo shivered again, pressing his back against me like a magnet was pulling him. "Yeah," he whispered. "The massage and everything feels really good."

To accentuate his comment, I ran my oil-slick hands over his shoulders and down the front of his chest. Muzo gasped. My fingers brushed past his nipples, earning a squirm and a squeak of pleasure. My hands paused at his belly, where a fluffy line of dark hair disappeared under the waistband of his pants. Muzo inhaled shakily and went taut.

"Are you gonna...?" he asked.

"I want to," I confirmed. "Do *you* want it?"

"Yes," he blurted. "Is that even a question?"

"I'll never touch you in ways you don't like. My only wish is to protect you and pleasure you in equal measure."

Muzo let out a blissful sigh as he relaxed his full weight against me. "Y'know, you should write a book or something. You have such a way with words. Even that card you wrote gave me the jitters, in a good way."

Now there was something I had never been told. People said I was blunt and straightforward, to the point of carelessness sometimes.

"Really?" I asked.

Muzo tilted his head back so he looked at me upside-down. "Yup. I think it's 'cause you're so honest. Your words come from the heart." He beamed, his smile reaching his eyes. "It's really sweet."

Fondness shone in Muzo's eyes. It struck a chord in my soul. We hadn't discussed being fated mates—I didn't even know if he realized it yet—but the love was there. It was in the way he looked at me with unconditional trust and honest affection.

With his head tilted back, he was at the perfect angle to kiss him. So I did.

I leaned down and pressed our mouths together. Muzo sighed into the kiss. The sensation of his warm breath over my sensitive lips made me shiver. I snaked my tongue into his mouth, gentle and probing. To my surprise, he met it with unbridled fervor. He'd gained enough confidence to kiss me passionately, to twist his slippery wet tongue against mine.

The kiss fanned the flames of my arousal. I was painfully hard—too hard to stand the confines of my pants anymore. Without breaking the kiss, I undid my belt and unzipped with one hand. I shoved my pants down past my hips so my cock was free to tent my briefs instead. Instant relief washed over me.

"Whoa," Muzo said. He stared over his shoulder, wide-eyed at the bulge in my underwear. A hungry look crept into his gaze.

But I wasn't done with him yet. He gave me permission to touch him, and I wasn't about to waste it.

While Muzo ogled me, I slipped my hand beneath his jeans. He let out a yelp that melted into a moan as my fingers brushed against his sensitive cock. He was hard, and though it was proportionate to his lithe body, his cock was much smaller than mine. I could fit his entire erection in my hand—which is exactly what I did.

Muzo's spine went rigid. He cried out, his back flush

against my chest. The delicious sound made my cock twitch.

"Does that feel good?" I asked.

He made an undecipherable noise accompanied by a firm nod. That was enough encouragement to continue. Muzo whined with need, cuddling up to me as I touched him. The warm weight of his body against my chest was delightful. I rearranged my position so my legs stretched out on either side of Muzo. He sat between them, fully engulfed by my presence. Safe. Secure.

"Cobalt," Muzo whimpered. The throaty hitch in his voice drove me wild. "You're gonna make me... y'know..."

My lips brushed his temple as I spoke. "Say it."

Muzo swallowed, his throat bobbing. "Gonna make me come."

I lowered my voice. "I *want* you to come."

A full-body shiver wracked Muzo. He tossed his head back with a high keening sound. My hand worked faster, speeding into a steady rhythm. My warm, oil-slick palm slid up and down his throbbing shaft. Each pump made Muzo hiss with pleasure. He twitched violently, pushing up against my chest as far as he'd go, as if trying to become one with me.

My dragon soul pulsed. I wanted to bite him —claim him.

Not yet.

I forced the urge to subside. Not until he realized he was my fated mate. Tonight was all about his pleasure. I had to prove to him how much I cared, how much I wanted him to be happy.

Muzo suddenly threw his arms up around my neck, clinging to me. His cock throbbed in my hand. He wasn't far from finishing. I quickened my pace, eager to see him come.

"Cobalt," he half-spoke, half-breathed. "I wanna kiss you."

I crushed my mouth against his. The kiss wasn't hungry—it was starving. I poured my alpha instincts into it, claiming Muzo's tongue with mine, showing him that he belonged to me and I to him.

Muzo's body went taut. The split-second of silence was broken as he screamed with pleasure into my mouth. I swallowed the sound eagerly. I didn't stop kissing him, or pumping his quivering cock. I wouldn't stop until the last drop of cum was spent.

When the last violent shudder passed, Muzo slumped against my chest. He panted hard, and his skin was drenched in sweat. I brushed the damp strands of black and blond hair from his forehead. His dark eyes sparkled with satisfaction, and an indescribable quality that looked a lot like love.

"You're like, really awesome," Muzo said, then flashed a sheepish grin. "Is that a weird thing to say after you just made me come?"

Warmth welled up in my chest. I kissed Muzo's forehead.

"No," I replied with a smile.

Muzo grinned back, then gasped. "Oh! I forgot." His gaze snapped down to my cock. He licked his lips. "Should I, uh..."

My pulse skyrocketed at the implication.

"If you want to," I rasped.

Muzo turned around, then held out his palm. "Oil me."

I handed him the bottle. Once he'd slicked up his hands, he reached beneath the stretched fabric and touched me. I groaned in pleasure. The sensation was unbelievable.

Muzo grinned. "Man, you're *huge*. I should've figured, since you're big in every other way."

He hooked a finger into my briefs and pulled them down, releasing my cock. He worked his hands up and down my length until it ached with need. My body trembled. I was no stranger to this feeling, but until now it came only from my own hand. Muzo's touch was something else. It felt so much better.

I was too worked up to last. A growl vibrated in my throat. My teeth transformed into fangs, grinding together with a sharp hiss. My dragon lurked right below the surface—he wanted me to sink my teeth into Muzo, plunge my cock into him, and breed him right here, right now.

But the anticipation would make our eventual mating all the sweeter.

Instead, my nails—which shifted into talons—raked the bed covers. I threw my head back with a feral roar as the orgasm ripped through me like a tidal wave. Muzo's oily hands kept working my cock as I came.

I exhaled a puff of smoke as the aftershocks slowly faded. My vision was blurry. My body was spent.

And I still wanted more.

Suddenly, Muzo grabbed me like I was an oversized doll and flopped backwards onto the bed. He beamed with a huge ecstatic grin, then snuggled up close. My draconic libido died down when I looked into his eyes.

Sex could wait. We had a lot of cuddling to do.

Before I could wrap my arms around him, Muzo cried, "Wait!" He grabbed the dragon plushie and cradled it against his chest. It was comically half his size. "There. Now all three of us can snuggle."

I raised a brow at the phrase *all three of us*. "I don't remember him being invited," I grumbled.

Muzo laughed. "Wait, are you seriously getting jealous of a plush toy?"

"I might be."

Muzo lifted the toy's head. Its delicate hand-embroidered eyes met my gaze, begging for mercy.

"Oh, please, Mr. Cobalt, please don't kick me out of the bed," Muzo said in a higher-pitched voice, speaking for the plushie.

I pouted. "The toy is a symbol of my dragon form. You can cuddle the real thing. Me."

Muzo laughed again. Apparently, he found this hilarious.

"C'mon, you don't want Blueberry to sleep with us tonight?" Muzo asked.

My second brow rose to join the first. "You named it? And the name isn't *Cobalt*?"

Muzo tilted his head, examining the toy. "He doesn't really look like a Cobalt, does he? Blueberry suits him much better. Besides, his round little snout kinda looks like a blueberry, doesn't it?"

I was starting to regret commissioning Taylor to sew the damned thing. But it was fine. It was worth it to see the joy on Muzo's face.

"Just remember Blueberry won't save you from drowning," I said, pulling him closer. "And my cock is bigger than his."

That made Muzo cackle. He nestled his face against my collarbone with Blueberry squished between our bodies. Maybe it wasn't so bad that he was there after all, as long as I got to sleep with Muzo tucked into my arms.

A knock came at the balcony door.

I frowned. My alpha instincts didn't warn me of danger, but I still didn't welcome the interruption.

"What the? Who could possibly visit at this hour?"

Muzo asked with a yawn. "And how the hell'd they get up there, anyway?"

My frown etched deeper. Unfortunately, I had a pretty good idea of who our visitor was.

I sighed, grudgingly getting off the bed. "Wait here."

Just as I expected, Jade stood on the balcony. He crossed his arms and tipped his head in an admonishing you-know-what-you-did way.

"Cobalt," he began.

My frown was about to become permanent. "Yes."

"You're not planning to accidentally fall asleep in Muzo's bed, are you?"

That was exactly what I planned on doing.

"Why shouldn't I?" I challenged.

Jade gestured calmly with his hand. "Because every time an alpha dragon bachelor stays with their mate overnight, there's a scandal the next morning. First it was Crimson causing a kerfuffle between Taylor and Alaric, and then Thystle overslept and missed the challenge he was supposed to be attending."

"I'm not like them," I said. "I'll wake up early and leave before I'm noticed."

"I'm sure that's what *they* intended, too," Jade pointed out. "But it's not easy to resist the call of your mate's arms, is it?"

I bit my lip. He wasn't wrong. I could've spent an eternity lying in bed with Muzo.

After Jade finished his sentence, Muzo plodded outside with another yawn. Blueberry was clutched firmly in his hand.

"What's goin' on?" he asked.

"Good evening, Muzo," Jade said with a polite smile. "I've come to gently scold Cobalt."

Muzo nodded, disappointed but understanding. "Oh.

Right, 'cause he's not technically supposed to be here, huh?"

"That's right."

To my surprise, Muzo grinned at me. "It's okay, Cobalt. I'll still be here tomorrow. And we still have the rest of the Games to be together."

Something struck me as odd in the way he said that, but I couldn't place why. Before I could analyze it, Jade's hand on my arm pulled me from my thoughts.

"One night's sleep apart. That's it. I'm sure you can manage that, hm?" Jade suggested.

I grunted. "Fine."

"Splendid. And thank you, Muzo, for your cooperation." Jade leaned on the balcony railing, ready to shift and fly back to the castle. "Coming, Cobalt?"

I glanced back at Muzo, who waved at me. That adorable mental image was enough to tide me over until the next morning—especially with the way he snuggled the blue dragon plushie close to his chest. Different name or not, it was still a symbol of me.

If I *had* to leave, then I was loath to do it without a goodnight kiss. I pressed a soft, quick kiss to Muzo's cheek before joining Jade in the starry night sky.

THIRTEEN

Muzo

I SPENT ABOUT two minutes being sad that Cobalt had to leave. Then the post-orgasm fatigue combined with the day's exhaustion hit me like an eighteen-wheeler truck, and I passed out.

The next morning, I was shovelling food onto my plate at the all-inclusive breakfast buffet when a hesitant finger tapped me on the shoulder. Poppy stood behind me with a shy smile.

"Oh, hey, Pops," I greeted, offering him a bite of my half-eaten roll. "Want some?"

"Ah, no, thank you."

I shrugged and tossed the other half into my mouth. "What's up?"

"How was your date with Cobalt last night?" he asked.

"It was awesome. I mean, I kinda screwed it up 'cause I ate a bunch of chocolate beforehand, but we still had a great time. He's really nice."

I didn't mention the part when he came over after and we gave each other hand jobs. That wasn't the type of thing you discussed over breakfast.

Poppy's smile brightened. "That's wonderful. I'm happy to hear that."

Alaric slipped into the conversation uninvited like a typical cat. "Once again, the wolf has forgotten this is a competition," he said, taking a sip of coffee.

Poppy turned sharply to Alaric. "I haven't forgotten!"

Both Alaric and I blinked in surprise at his outburst. That was a big reaction to one of Alaric's run-of-the-mill sassy comments.

Realizing he'd raised his voice an inch, Poppy shrank. "Sorry. I didn't mean to shout."

Alaric snorted. "If that's shouting, then the jackal's regular speaking volume is louder than a jet engine." He took another sip. "In any case, the bachelor clearly has no interest in either of us."

Poppy's eyes flashed with hope. "You really think so?"

"I know so." Alaric arched a brow. "Although I fail to see why you're so chuffed about being a loser."

"I'm not," Poppy argued weakly.

"Sure. And I'm a Siamese." Alaric sighed, rubbing his temple. "Honest to gods, if the producers drag us through every season of this show and I *don't* end up with a mate at the end..."

I munched on a strip of bacon as they went back and forth. For once, I agreed with Alaric. Why wasn't Poppy invested in winning? He was a nice, sweet omega. He should have an equal chance with Cobalt.

Then a sharp, twisting pain stabbed my chest and I nearly dropped my bacon.

What the hell was that? Did I not want Poppy to be with Cobalt?

For the sake of experiment, I imagined the two of them together. This time, I actually *did* drop my bacon.

No, I realized. I didn't want anybody else to be with Cobalt except me.

The sensation was alien and bizarre. I wasn't usually selfish. I never felt owed anything. But when it came to Cobalt, I distinctly didn't want to share. I wanted him all to myself.

Weird.

"Um, Muzo? You dropped this," Poppy said, picking up the bacon.

Alaric pulled a face. "Please tell me you're not going to eat that."

"Five second rule," I announced, snatching the floor bacon and tossing it in my mouth.

"WELCOME, OMEGAS, TO THE SECOND CHALLENGE!" Gaius announced.

We gathered at a stream at the base of an inlet, where the water met the forest, and the sandy beach turned to shrubs and trees. Gaius and Cobalt stood at the opposite end of the stream.

My heart did a back flip at the sight of him. I hadn't realized how much I'd missed Cobalt. It was only one sleep and a couple hours apart, sure, but it still felt too long. No wonder he didn't want to leave last night. It would've been nice if we'd spent the night together.

"I bet you're wondering what your task is today," Gaius went on. His shirt was neon orange today. He put high-lighters everywhere to shame. "Well, I'm glad you asked. You'll be playing a game called Catch the Catch! You'll need to *catch* something that *catches* the bachelor's eye."

"That is an absolutely heinous name," Alaric mumbled next to me.

"I think it's neat," I whispered back.

Alaric looked like he was about to gag on a hairball.

"You're free to gather whatever you like," Gaius explained. "Plants, animals, rocks; water, land, sky, dirt— it's all fair game. Use your imagination!"

Alaric rolled his eyes. "Oh, goody. Another subjective challenge. I wonder who will win this time," he added, shooting me a glance.

Why did he do that?

"I have the same chance of winning as everyone else," I said.

Alaric shrugged. "Keep telling yourself that."

Confused, I glanced across the stream at Cobalt. He stared directly at me with a slight smile in the corner of his mouth. His gaze was attentive, rapt—like nobody else even existed.

My heart fluttered.

Was Alaric right about me winning? But that didn't make any sense. That meant Cobalt thought I was special, that he liked me the most...

My pulse raced as I remembered last night's date and our spicy evening visit. I swallowed at the memory and mentally swatted it away before I got a boner again.

Cobalt obviously wasn't doing those things with other people. His gestures were sweet, his words sweeter, and he always went out of his way to please me. Almost like he was trying to prove something…

Across the stream, Gaius nudged Cobalt with his elbow and nodded towards the hotel. Cobalt frowned deeply. I couldn't hear what they were saying, but it seemed like Gaius was telling Cobalt he had to leave. Maybe the producers didn't want Cobalt present since he'd interfered during the last challenge. I thought about what Alaric said —would Cobalt help me win if he stayed?

He'd really do that for me...?

But it was no use challenging the host. As Cobalt flashed the biggest pout known to man, Gaius nodded sympathetically and urged him away. Before Cobalt stomped off, he glanced over his shoulder at me, his blue eyes clouded with longing.

I smiled to reassure him. I had a feeling we wouldn't be apart for too long.

I was so busy watching Cobalt walk away that I didn't pay attention to Gaius's spiel. All of a sudden, I heard him call: "Ready, omegas? Go!"

Everyone scattered. Some omegas ran off in their human forms, others as animals. Meanwhile, I stood there like a lump, not knowing what to do. The sudden realization about Cobalt flustered me. I had no idea where to begin for this challenge.

"Muzo!" Poppy cried.

I glanced down to see him in his wolf form. The fur on the back of his neck ruffled with excitement, or nerves. Knowing Poppy, it was probably the latter.

"I have an idea," Poppy said. "A bunch of omegas are hunting for prey in the forest, but I don't think that's right. Remember how the first challenge was about water? I think this one is, too. We should try fishing in the stream."

"We?" Alaric interjected. "I wasn't aware this was a group activity."

Poppy's ears flattened as he glared at Alaric. Which was unusual because Poppy never glared at anybody. What was up with him lately?

"We've helped each other in challenges before," Poppy pointed out.

Alaric sniffed and turned to leave. "Suit yourselves. I'm not about to get my hands dirty for a challenge I have no possibility of winning. If you need me, I'll be tanning on the beach."

"Forget him," Poppy insisted. "We can do this together."

It was rare to see him so determined, so I didn't want to turn down his offer, though I still didn't understand his uncharacteristic ambition.

"Sure, Pops, if that's what you want," I said.

He nodded, relieved, then hunkered down by the stream about ten feet away. "You start there, I'll start here, and we'll meet in the middle."

"Okay."

Poppy instantly got to work. His eyes scanned the rushing water, his paw at the ready to catch a fish.

I stared into the stream. The flow calmed me. I could've shut my eyes and listened to the peaceful running water until I fell asleep.

But it wasn't the time or place for that. I wanted to try my best to win the challenge on my own terms, no matter what Alaric said. If Cobalt chose me as the winner, I'd be happy.

If he didn't, then…

My skin prickled with unease. Actually, I didn't *want* to think about Cobalt picking a different winner.

I kneeled at the edge of the stream in human form, my fingers curling into the earth. Unlike Alaric, I didn't care if I got dirty, especially if it resulted in another shower session with Cobalt.

Ugh, I couldn't think about that stuff right now. Getting a boner was not conducive to fishing.

"I got one!" Poppy cried, his voice muffled by a big fish clenched in his jaws.

He looked ecstatic, but the fish had other ideas. It thrashed for dear life, slapping Poppy's muzzle with its tail until it broke free. Poppy yelped as the fish disappeared back into the stream.

"Catch it, Muzo!" he cried.

Even if I wanted to catch the fish, it was too late. The aquatic escapee sped past me and my clumsy human hands, disappearing downstream.

Poppy ran over to me with a crease in his brows. "Why did you let it go? It might've helped you win."

I shook my head. "Thanks, Pops, but I want to do this on my own. I'm gonna prove to Alaric that I can win fair and square."

Poppy's ears flattened. He looked uncomfortable, like he was struggling not to argue with me.

"What's up with you lately?" I asked. "You've been acting weird since we got here."

Poppy's pelt prickled. "No, I haven't."

"Uh, yeah, you have."

He licked the fur on his chest distractedly. "A-anyway, we shouldn't waste time. I'm gonna catch another fish."

"And give it to me?" I accused.

Poppy's eyes widened like saucers. "No!"

I grasped either side of his furry head. "Poppy Faolan, did you just tell a lie?"

Poppy whimpered like I'd stepped on his paw. He looked ready to faint. I suddenly felt bad, so I backed off.

"Sorry, Pops," I said. "I'm not trying to agitate you. I just want you to tell the truth."

The next words out of Poppy's mouth sounded like they'd been boiling for days. "Then so should you," he muttered.

"What?"

Poppy anxiously peeked over his shoulder at the camera crew. "I don't want to say it in front of everyone," he murmured. "But... you know. Your situation."

It finally dawned on me. *That's* why Poppy was so worried. That was why he kept pushing me to do well and assisting me during challenges at his own expense.

Because if I lost the Dragonfate Games this time, I had nothing to go back to. No home. No job.

No mate.

A wave of emotion hit me. I wrapped my arms around Poppy's fluffy neck in a big hug.

"Oh, Pops," I murmured into his fur. "You're the sweetest friend a guy could ask for, y'know that?"

A soft whine escaped him. "I just want you to be safe..."

"I *am* safe."

His voice quivered. "I don't mean right now. I mean after the Games. When we go back to reality. I'm not supposed to have people over in my apartment, but if we're careful, you can stay with me. But my place is so small, and my job barely covers my bills. I don't know if I can feed both of us..."

"Whoa, whoa, slow down," I said. I stroked the top of his head, hoping to calm him down. "Don't worry about all that now. We're supposed to be on vacation."

Tears formed in Poppy's big, brown eyes. "How can I not worry? I can't relax when you're—" His voice broke. "Homeless..."

"Everything's gonna be okay," I promised with a smile. I didn't know how or why, but I believed it to my very core. What I told Poppy was the truth.

He gave me a curious look with his doe eyes. "Cobalt likes you, right?"

"Sure does." I grinned. "In ways I haven't even told you about yet."

Poppy lifted his head, his ears perking forward. "Really?"

"Uh huh. So, don't sweat it." I nodded at the stream. "Let's catch something, okay?"

He sniffled. "Okay."

I crouched by the stream and scanned the water. Fish darted past, but none of them caught my eye. I heard Poppy splashing upstream. He must've been trying to catch as many as possible.

Glancing past the fish, I searched the stream bed. Silt and rocks dotted the calm, motionless floor. It looked so peaceful down there.

Slowly, I reached my hand inside. I ignored the panicked fish giving me a wide berth. Closing my eyes, I trailed my fingers along the bottom. I experienced a flash of feeling, of being spiritually close to Cobalt.

My fingers hit something solid. I paused. It was about the size of my fist with a hard surface, like a rock.

When I opened my eyes, I felt an unexpected powerful flash of nostalgia.

It wasn't a rock—it was a shell. The beautifully spiralled shell of a snail. The modest gray and brown stripes blending into the stream bed in the perfect camouflage.

I stared at it in fuzzy recognition. Where had I seen this snail before?

As the memory suddenly unfurled in my mind, I sucked in a soft breath. That fateful day in the ocean, way back when...

I shuddered, then smiled at the snail. I didn't know why, but I felt as if Cobalt would like it, too. I gently picked it up and placed it in the bucket with some water from its home.

Poppy bounded over. "Muzo, you caught something! What is it?"

I proudly showed him the bucket. "Look!"

When he peered inside, his fur flattened in disappointment. "Oh. It's... just a snail?"

"It's not just a snail," I said, shaking my head. "There's something special about it. I feel it in my gut."

Poppy didn't seem convinced, but tried to keep an optimistic expression. "Well, it's a good start. Let's keep trying."

He went back to fishing, but I was finished. I had the only catch I needed.

"Hey, little guy," I whispered to the snail. "You and me —we're gonna win this challenge. I just know it."

The snail wiggled its antennae.

FOURTEEN

Cobalt

THE LAST PLACE I wanted to be right now was trapped in a hotel office with the twins.

My leg bounced impatiently. After my brief appearance at the start of the challenge, I was ushered away against my will. Apparently, my presence might've influenced the contestants' decisions, and Jade thought the challenges would seem fairer if I wasn't there fawning over Muzo the entire time.

I suppose he had a point.

I sighed in frustration, sinking back in my chair. The longer the Games went on, the more I agreed with Crimson's initial disdain for them—it *was* a whole lot of bullshit.

I wasn't left completely in the dark, though. The producers provided a TV in the office airing a live stream of the challenge so I could watch it from a distance. The footage was only meant for me, but the twins were famously nosy. They snuck into the office before I even showed up, so I didn't bother kicking them out—even if they *were* blocking half the TV.

Aurum and Saffron crouched shoulder-to-shoulder in

front of the screen, loudly narrating and commenting on everything like they were watching a football game.

Out of all my younger brothers, the twins felt the hardest to reach emotionally. Ever since they hatched from the same egg, they'd lived in their own little bubble, always preferring each other's company to the rest of the world. They respected me as the eldest dragon, but at the end of the day, each other's input was more important.

To be honest, I worried for them. How would they find fated mates if they were constantly attached at the hip? The Dragonfate Games were originally Saffron's idea, so I assumed he wanted a mate, but Aurum only showed interest in watching the Games, not participating.

"Dude, are you seeing Alaric right now?" Aurum asked. "He's straight up tanning during the challenge."

Saffron snorted. "He needs one. He's paler than a ghost."

"Harsh. But true."

It was safe to say neither of them were fated to Alaric. I obviously wasn't, either. From what I could see over the twins' matching golden heads, the cameraman was interviewing Alaric on the beach. I wished the live feed would pan away from him already.

"He's the one, right, Cobalt?" Aurum asked with a snarky grin.

"No," I growled.

They snickered among themselves.

"We already know which one *you* like," Saffron said smugly. "His name starts with M and ends with *uzo.*"

"Yeah, he likes the one who almost drowned." Aurum rolled his eyes. "I still don't know how that showed off his water affinity, but whatever."

The hairs on the back of my neck bristled. "You wouldn't understand," I said quietly.

"Yeah. I don't. That's literally what I just said, bro."

"He would've done fine if the other contestants didn't interfere," I insisted.

It didn't bother me that Aurum didn't understand. I saw something different than everyone else that day—something only I would've noticed.

Aurum shrugged dismissively. "I dunno. I just think you can do better, Cobalt."

Saffron started, his eyes widening. "Dude. You can't say that."

Frowning, Aurum met his twin's shocked gaze. "Why? It's my opinion."

"Still," Saffron argued, now sporting a frown of his own.

"What? I'm not saying he shouldn't like the guy, I just said he could do better—in *my* opinion," Aurum repeated.

The sudden tension in the air gave me pause. The twins rarely argued, but they'd been doing it more often since the Dragonfate Games first started. Saffron was always the sensitive one while Aurum leaned more devil-may-care, but their differences intensified when it came to love. It was strange and uncomfortable to see them disagree.

"It's fine, Saffron," I said to diffuse the situation. "I'm not offended."

Aurum took that as a win. He puffed out his chest. "See?"

"Hmph," Saffron muttered, facing the screen again.

The awkward blip faded as the twins got absorbed in the live stream again. I didn't care what happened on the screen unless Muzo was involved, so I laid back in my chair and shut my eyes. Jade must've directed the camera crew to capture more footage of the other contestants so they'd have enough diversity for the final cut.

I couldn't have given less of a shit about the TV show. I just wanted my mate. Wasn't that the point of all of this?

"Cobalt, you have a scary expression right now," Saffron said hesitantly. "You okay?"

I peeked an eye open. "I do?"

"It's just his resting alpha face," Aurum remarked. "He's probably pissed he's not macking on Muzo right now."

"I am," I stated.

Aurum shook his head. "I don't get that. You seriously can't handle spending, what, an hour or two apart?"

Aside from his usual tone, his question sounded genuine. But the longer I spent in this office, the thinner my patience wore. Aurum's comment grated on my nerves.

"When it happens to you, then you'll understand," I assured.

Aurum barked a derisive laugh. "Yeah, no. That won't be happening to me."

Saffron stared at him again. I did the same. The office went uncomfortably silent for a beat.

"What?" Aurum asked. "You guys are looking at me like I said the worst thing imaginable."

"What do you mean, it won't happen to you?" Saffron demanded. "Are you, like, worried that it won't?"

"No. I just don't care," Aurum said bluntly. "Now can we get back to the stream?"

But Saffron looked frazzled. "What do you *mean* you don't—"

Suddenly, a flash of black and blond hair caught my eye. Muzo was on screen.

I bolted from my chair. In my excitement, I accidentally shouldered the twins aside. They fell over like a pair of bowling pins.

"Hey!" Aurum cried.

Saffron gasped, pointing at the screen. "Look, there he is!"

Aurum grumbled as he pushed himself back into a sitting position. "Was it worth giving me a concussion?"

"Sorry," I said.

My heart pounded. Just the sight of Muzo on screen ignited my passion for him. I cursed Jade's restrictive rules. I should've been there to cheer on my mate, not stuck in this office.

The live stream showed Muzo in human form speaking to his friend Poppy as a wolf. The feed was synced up with their mics, but Poppy spoke so meekly it was difficult to hear him.

"See? That wolf's pretty cute. Why not go for him instead?" Aurum suggested.

"Be quiet," Saffron and I snapped at the same time.

Aurum scoffed. "Bro, now you're twinning with Cobalt instead of me? Not cool."

My patience ground down to a single molecule. I whipped my gaze to Aurum.

"I am trying to hear my mate speak," I growled. "If you're going to talk over him, then you can leave. Is that clear?"

I must have looked terrifying because fear flashed across Aurum's face before he snorted and got up.

"Fine," he muttered. "You two watch by yourselves since you're so close. I'm out of here."

Saffron frowned. "Wait, Aurum—"

But his twin had left already, slamming the door behind him. In any other circumstances, I would've chased after him to make sure he was okay, but I couldn't tear my attention from Muzo.

Something was happening on-screen. It looked like the friends were having a disagreement. But over what? Poppy was submissive and gentle, and Muzo always went with the flow. Neither omega argued easily.

I had a bad feeling about it. I held my breath, leaning closer to the screen.

Then, Poppy said the word that stopped my heart.

Homeless.

Time slowed around me. I forgot how to breathe.

At first, I didn't know what to think. It couldn't be true, could it?

But Muzo didn't deny it.

Something grabbed my wrist. It snapped me out of my daze.

Saffron stared at me in disbelief. "Cobalt, did you hear that?" he asked hurriedly. "Are they serious?"

A cold feeling shimmied down my spine, then froze in the pit of my stomach. I recalled the unexplained sharp, stabbing pains in my chest—the ones that stopped when I finally came face-to-face with Muzo.

My dragon rumbled within me, encroaching on my consciousness.

I had to go to my mate.

As soon as I stood, I lurched to one side. My dragon's weight was too much for my current body. I pushed against the wall with my hand to stop myself from falling. I gritted my teeth with a sharp hiss. My dragon raged against the barrier separating us.

This revelation was too much to take. He wanted out.

"Cobalt?" Saffron asked. "You okay?"

His voice sounded distant, like it was coming from a different room.

I had to maintain control. If I lost it and shifted now, I'd crush Saffron and destroy the entire hotel.

I bit down on my tongue hard enough to taste copper. The sudden pain diverted my attention for a few moments.

It afforded me enough time to bolt out of the room and make it outside the hotel.

As I gulped down the fresh air, I already felt the hard ridges of my dragon's spine bubbling beneath my human back. I gasped, falling forward on all fours on the ground, panting hard. The hot sand spiked into my palms—another distracting bite of pain.

With eyes clamped shut, I breathed through the instinctive urge to shift.

Not yet. Not now. Get to Muzo first.

I hauled myself upright, then ran towards the inlet. Every footstep sank deeper in the sand than normal. My dragon's weight was still there, a reminder of his bid for freedom.

Blood pounded in my ears as I reached Muzo. He kneeled by the edge of the stream, his arms wet from the elbows down. Poppy was next to him. Upon my approach, I noticed the camera crew edging closer in my peripheral vision. I didn't want them present for this conversation. I steeled myself.

"Muzo," I said under my breath.

Muzo jumped excitedly at the sound of my voice. His face lit up. "Cobalt! You came back!"

The pure joy he radiated soothed my dragon's fury. Slightly.

Poppy's fur stood on end. He turned around with wide eyes, but didn't interrupt.

"I need a moment with you, Muzo. Alone," I muttered. I wasn't trying to sound angry, but with my towering position and shaky voice, I was afraid I might've seemed that way.

Thankfully, Muzo never misunderstood my intentions. He tilted his head. "Sure. Oh, lemme grab my bucket."

He picked up the handle and followed me towards the

edge of the forest. The hairs on the back of my neck prickled. My skin felt tight. I didn't know how much longer I
could contain my dragon.

The camera crew toddled along behind us, but as we
reached the treeline, I whipped around to glower at them.

"Stay where you are," I growled.

They exchanged confused glances. I was the big boss. I
paid their salaries. They were trying to do their jobs, but
now I was ordering them not to.

I didn't care that the entire show was meant to be
filmed—I needed to speak with Muzo privately. The whole
world didn't need to be part of this conversation.

Besides, if my dragon broke free, the crew could easily
film from a distance.

Muzo paused, unsure. "Not that I don't love getting
whisked away by you, but, uh, what about the challenge?"

"This will only take a minute."

"Okie doke."

The two of us—and Muzo's bucket—stopped in a
clearing in the forest. A chill rolled down my skin. A storm
was about to break.

There was no good way to bring it up, so I just started.

"I overheard you talking to Poppy on the live stream," I
said.

Muzo's mouth pulled into a frown. "Oh." He hung his
head. "You heard, huh?"

I didn't like seeing him shrink into himself. He was
already so small. I stepped closer and put my hands on his
arms, clutching him dearly.

"Why didn't you tell me?" I asked.

Muzo bit his lip. "About the not-having-an-apartment-
anymore thing?"

Pain stabbed my heart just thinking about it. "Yes."

Muzo's gaze fell to the ground. "I was having such a

good time. I didn't want to bring it up 'cause I didn't wanna worry you. Besides, I'd figure it out on my own. No need to burden anyone else with my problems, right?"

He didn't want to worry me.

He didn't want to be a burden.

My fated mate kept his problems to himself—because he didn't yet know I was *his* fated mate.

My skin rippled with barely contained power. My dragon let loose a primal roar in my soul, then finally snapped the restraints holding him back.

FIFTEEN

Muzo

I CLUTCHED my bucket and its contents for dear life as Cobalt transformed.

The towering alpha in front of me disappeared in a split-second. His presence exploded like a starburst, expanding into a massive, hulking form.

Calling Cobalt's dragon *big* was an understatement. He was tall as a three-story building, and his sprawling wing-span made him seem even larger. Long whiskers trailed from his face, and a silky blue mane flowed down his spine like a waterfall. His talons sank into the earth, gleaming like obsidian knives.

When the dust settled and his shift was over, I'd somehow landed on my butt with the bucket in my lap.

When I stared up at him in awe, the air left my lungs.

The dragon before my eyes felt unreal, like he'd been picked out of a fairy tale and dropped into real life. Each one of his overlapping scales glittered brighter than sapphires. Just like his hair in human form, Cobalt's hide ranged in shades of blue. His extremities were deeper blue, like the depths of the ocean; the main parts of his body were a rich royal blue, and his belly was the color of the morning sky.

He was so freaking gorgeous.

"Whoa," I said, at a loss for words.

Cobalt lowered his head, which was the size of a couch. His streaming whiskers tickled my outstretched legs.

His reptilian nostrils flared as he blew out a soft exhale. "I apologize. I couldn't contain myself any longer."

I laughed, putting my hands on the sides of his face. "What are you sorry for? You're amazing, Cobalt!"

A low sound rumbled in his throat like the world's deepest purr. He closed his eyes contentedly, his long lashes brushing against his cheeks.

"What's with the sudden shift? Is something wrong?" I asked. He'd seemed upset earlier. Was that what triggered his transformation?

Cobalt's beautiful eyes opened again. They were bottomless liquid pools with rings of neon blue.

"You told me the other night that I had a way with words," he began. "But I'm not the best at expressing myself. There is something I should've told you sooner."

I tilted my head. "If it's that you're a gigantic dragon, then I already know about that. But phew, seeing it up close and personal is really something else."

An amused huff escaped Cobalt's nostrils. "Not that." He went quiet and solemn before speaking again. "A few weeks before you came to the island, I sensed your pain. Every time life hurt you, I felt it. Here."

He raised a paw and placed it on his chest. Even though he was massive and his claws were terrifyingly sharp, the motion exuded unbelievable tenderness.

"A few weeks before," I echoed, remembering the string of unfortunate events. "That was when I got evicted, and then lost my job right after."

A growl like an earthquake reverberated in Cobalt's throat. It was so strong, it shook the ground beneath me.

"I was terrified," Cobalt admitted.

It was odd to hear that from his dragon's mouth. Such a huge, powerful creature shouldn't be afraid of anything. But he was... because of me.

Guilt washed over me again. This was the same thing that happened with Poppy. I didn't want to keep hurting the people I cared about.

"I'm sorry," I murmured, stroking the sides of his head. His scales were cool to the touch. "I never want anyone to feel bad 'cause of me. Especially not the people I love."

Cobalt's eyes flashed like lightning. His body went incredibly still—even his mane stopped flowing.

He parted his jaws slowly, revealing rows of fangs. He looked like he wanted to say something.

"Muzo, I—"

Suddenly, Gaius burst into the clearing with a gaggle of camera crew members in tow. The kobolds spread around us in a semi-circle, eager to catch us on film.

"And here we find the dragon in his natural habitat," Gaius announced, shattering the quiet. "Which is, apparently, having a one-on-one conversation with a contestant."

Cobalt's mane spiked into hackles. Tension rippled across his scales and his spine arched in anger.

"What are you doing here?" Cobalt growled at Gaius. The tenderness in his voice was gone.

Gaius sauntered up to the dragon without hesitation. He was lucky to be a close family friend—I got the feeling that was the only reason Cobalt didn't bite his neon shirt clean off.

"You know the drill by now," Gaius chided. "You do your thing, we capture footage for the show. You can't just run off on your own. The cameras see all," he said, wriggling his fingers.

Cobalt glared at him.

Gaius ignored the infuriated colossus behind him and summoned the cameras closer. He put his arm around me, pulling me into the shot. I grinned and waved.

"Well, folks, the Dragonfate Games are always full of surprises," Gaius said to the camera in his best hostly voice. "I sure didn't expect to see our bachelor go full dragon during the second challenge!" He thrust the mic into Cobalt's snout. "What made you shift, Cobalt? Did this contestant surprise and thrill you with his contribution to Catch the Catch?"

I wondered if that was Gaius's way of throwing him a bone. Clearly, Cobalt had no interest in the actual challenge, and Gaius must've realized the shift had nothing to do with it. But this way, he made them seem connected for the audience.

"Yes," Cobalt said slowly. I think he noticed Gaius's intervention too, because it shaved the edge off his irritation.

Gaius nodded. "What you're saying is, you were *so* impressed by Muzo's catch that you couldn't contain your draconic shift."

"That's right," Cobalt rumbled.

"Brilliant! There you have it, folks. If there's one sure-fire way to decide the winner of a challenge, a spontaneous dragon emergence is it!"

By now, the rest of the contestants noticed something was up. I mean, they couldn't *not* notice the skyscraper of a dragon in the vicinity. They crept to the edge of the clearing in various forms, still holding their buckets—although some of them had been dropped in shock at the sight of Cobalt's massive form. For a lot of the other omegas, it was their first time seeing the real him.

Well, his body, anyway. I was pretty sure only I knew the real him, inside *and* out.

Two familiar white-haired figures caught my eye. Poppy and Alaric were among the gathered contestants, both in human form now. Poppy lit up, barely containing his enthusiasm, while Alaric examined the non-existent tan on his arms.

"So, Muzo," Gaius said with a grin. "Care to share what your big catch is? The catch that impressed our bachelor *this* much?" He gestured to Cobalt's sweeping form.

In the chaos, I'd forgotten to show Cobalt my treasure. "Oh, yeah!"

Cobalt's long whiskers twitched. He angled his great head curiously. "What did you find?" he asked.

All eyes—and cameras—were on me. I stuck my hand into the bottom of the bucket and pulled out my catch. The snail's wet brown and gray shell gleamed in the reflected sunlight.

Cobalt's liquid eyes widened.

Everybody else squinted at the snail. Their confusion was palpable. I heard some contestants mutter that there must've been some kind of mistake.

"Ah," Gaius said, enthusiasm faltering. "That's... What exactly *is* that?"

It was Cobalt's growl-laced voice that broke in.

"That's a Chromatimaeus brackish river snail," he uttered. His tone was grave, yet brimming with hope. "They're a rare species that only exists on this island. But I haven't seen another one in over a decade. I... I thought they were extinct in the wild. Muzo, I can't believe you actually found one."

Hearing the excitement in Cobalt's voice excited me,

too. I broke into a huge grin. "I *knew* there was something special about this little guy!"

Suddenly, I felt a long, cool sensation brush against me. I glanced down to see the tip of Cobalt's tail curling against my legs. His eyes blazed with emotion as he stared me down. The intensity of his gaze sent a shiver across my skin. It was like Gaius, the crew, and the other contestants didn't even exist. I was the only thing in Cobalt's whole world.

I put the snail safely back in the bucket. Gaius was saying something about a winner's date in the background, but I wasn't really paying attention because Cobalt reached his large paw towards me. A second later, I was gently clutched within it.

His booming command rang out: "Everybody back up."

Everybody stumbled out of the way as Cobalt pumped his wings and pushed against the ground at the same time. He heaved upward with grace I'd never expect from such a huge body. Once he cleared the tops of the trees, he flapped his wings. The gusts born from his wing beats whooshed across the canopy, making all the leaves dance.

The wind whipped my face as Cobalt soared higher. I cried out in unabashed laughter.

We were freaking *flying*.

"Whoo!" I screamed with joy. Then, remembering the precious cargo, I clutched the bucket closer to my chest, the same way Cobalt held me to his chest. Thankfully, the snail was stuck to the bottom.

Cobalt was one with the sky. I eagerly looked around. Everything, everywhere, as far as I could see was blue. The sky, the ocean, and Cobalt's scales. I relaxed in his grip as I enjoyed the view. Whoever said blue was a calming color wasn't lying.

It wasn't a long flight. Soon Cobalt landed in front of a beautiful castle, then placed me gently on my feet. He patted me on the head with his paw and smoothed out the windswept explosion that was my hair.

"We're home," Cobalt stated, already walking ahead.

That specific word caught me off guard. I stopped. "Home?"

He looked over his shoulder. "Yes. Our home."

For one wild second, I wondered if he meant me and him, but then I figured he meant his brothers—his actual blood family.

I followed him inside the yawning front doors. It shouldn't have surprised me that everything was dragon-sized. Here, away from humans, the dragon shifters could live however they wanted. That sounded so freeing. Nobody could evict *them* from their house because of any pet clauses.

I craned my neck back to stare at all the ceiling details. The castle was a bit overwhelming.

"Are you all right, Muzo?" Cobalt asked when I hadn't moved.

"Yeah," I said. "Just thinking about how you could fit, like, a million of my apartment in the front hallway alone." I paused, then corrected myself. "Uh, former apartment."

Cobalt's mane bristled like icicle shards before settling again. He reached his paw towards me. "Come. I want to show you something."

I stepped closer, letting Cobalt hold me like he'd done in the sky. I had to say, being snuggled against a dragon's chest was truly the superior way to travel. It was so relaxing that my eyes lulled shut.

When Cobalt suddenly paused at the top of the stairs, I opened my eyes to an unexpected sight. A tall alpha dressed in dark leather blocked our path. His hair was a deep shade of purple, almost iridescent black. He sat on the final step, as if waiting for Cobalt's arrival. His piercing eyes flashed upon seeing me.

Math was never my strong suit, but I tried calculating it in my head. How many colors were there in a rainbow again? If there were seven alpha dragons, and this purple guy clearly wasn't the *other* purple alpha Thystle, then who was he?

The alpha nodded at me. "That him?" he asked Cobalt roughly.

"Yes," Cobalt replied. His deep dragon voice filled the stairwell. As he spoke, his paw clutched tighter around me. It didn't hurt, but it was enough that I noticed it.

The purple alpha grunted and stood up. "Good," he muttered. "Congrats."

Despite the alpha's gruff tone, I noticed he sounded oddly relieved. I glanced up at Cobalt. "Are you two having a fight or something?" I asked.

Cobalt's paw relaxed. "No," he said after a moment.

The alpha snorted. "That's a nice way of saying we *had* a fight, but we're cool now. And since he won't introduce me, I'll do it myself. I'm Viol. You must be Muzo."

"Viol!" I said in a eureka moment. "Like violet, right? That's the color I couldn't figure out."

Viol's mouth curved into a wry smirk. "No, not like violet." As he grinned, dragon fangs filled his human mouth. "Like *violence*."

"Whoa," I murmured. "Cool."

Viol grinned. "I like this one already."

"Not cool. Edgy and unnecessary," Cobalt grumbled. "If you'll excuse us, Viol."

Viol sauntered out of the way. He grabbed the railing, casually leapt over it, then shifted half-way down.

Cobalt huffed and marched down the hall before I could see the rest. "Don't mind him."

"Who's minding? I think he's cool," I said.

I felt the immediate rumbling growl in Cobalt's chest.

"Not cooler than you, obviously," I corrected, grinning up at him. "I'll always think you're the best, Cobalt."

He paused. "Do you mean that?"

"Duh. You're only the biggest, nicest, most thoughtful and awesome dragon I've ever met."

His maw curled into a smile. For a dragon, he was oddly expressive.

When we reached a nondescript door, Cobalt finally shifted back to human form. I still felt as safe and warm in his arms as I did in his paws, but now he was noticeably naked. Too bad I couldn't check him out properly since I was curled up bridal-style.

Cobalt carried me into a shockingly simple room. A king-sized bed, a dresser, and a desk were the only pieces of furniture. The back wall was a window that overlooked the ocean. There was nothing overt in the room that screamed 'Cobalt.'

"This is your room?" I asked.

"Yes."

Before I could probe further, he plopped me on the bed while he rummaged through the dresser. He threw on a simple white T-shirt that showed off his muscular arms and a pair of dark blue jeans that showed off his shapely ass—I mean, nope, definitely wasn't checking out his butt.

Dressed now, Cobalt walked towards the far wall. "Come with me."

"Sure," I said. "But, uh, where exactly are we going?"

I only saw three plain walls, plus the huge glass window. As far as I could tell, there wasn't anywhere *to* go.

In any case, I followed Cobalt. He stood in front of a

wall. Was he going to meditate into another dimension or something?

But then I noticed a subtle handle blending into the wall. There was a door right in front of me and I hadn't even noticed it.

"Whoa," I said excitedly. "Cobalt, you have a secret lair?"

The corner of his mouth lifted in a smile. "Kind of."

He pushed the door open. Blue light flooded into the room like a beacon.

"Welcome to my hoard, Muzo."

SIXTEEN

Cobalt

I HAD NEVER BEFORE LET anybody into my inner sanctum.

But now, it was time.

Muzo's jaw dropped as he stepped into the chamber. His pupils dilated as they adjusted to the difference in light. He looked like a statue as he clutched the bucket and stared into the water-filled glass enclosure surrounding us. It spanned from floor to ceiling, stretching across all four walls.

My hoard wasn't *in* the room—it *was* the room.

"Is this... an aquarium?" Muzo breathed.

"You could say that," I agreed.

Muzo stepped closer to the glass, then paused. "Can I touch it?"

"Yes."

He placed his hand on the tank. Dappled light reflected off his face. His eyes shined bright with wonder. Just past the glass, huge strands of kelp slow-danced in the water. Little shrimp dug in the sandy substrate. Pencil-sized silver fish swam by in schools, and other tiny particles of life floated by.

Muzo was strangely silent.

I felt apprehensive waiting for his response. Was he entranced? Or was he trying to think of something nice to say?

It wasn't a conventional dragon hoard. I knew that. That was why I kept it to myself. It meant too much to me to bring up in conversations for fear of ridicule. I'd rather keep it a secret than open myself up to negativity.

But Muzo was my fated mate. I cared about his opinion more than anybody else's—and if I couldn't tell my fated mate about my hoard, who *could* I tell?

"My brothers have never seen my hoard," I said quietly. "You're the only person I've allowed in here."

Muzo didn't turn around. "Just me?" he asked quietly.

I swallowed the nervous lump in my throat. "Yes."

He didn't say anything else. He just stared into the water.

I clutched my chest. This feeling wasn't wrong. Muzo *was* my fated mate. But that didn't mean he'd love my hoard the same way I did. He was his own person, with his own opinions. He could've hated water for all I knew.

With a flash of shame, I remembered that Muzo nearly drowned earlier. Was his silence from fear? Was bringing him here a mistake?

"I'm sorry, Muzo," I said hurriedly. "I shouldn't have—"

"I remember this place," Muzo said softly.

I froze.

What did he mean by that? He'd never been in this chamber before. That was a fact. Since my brothers weren't allowed here either, there was no way photos of it could've leaked.

As my mind raced with doubts and questions, Muzo turned around. Tears wet his eyes, but he didn't look sad.

"I've seen this before," Muzo insisted.

That was impossible.

Yet something in his expression gave me pause. There was a nostalgic lustre in his gaze.

He wasn't lying about this.

I walked closer, standing by his side at the tank, then asked, "How?"

Muzo blinked at the kelp before letting out a long, deep sigh, like he'd been holding his breath for ages.

"Y'know how I lost my apartment and my job?" he asked.

I ground my teeth remembering the world's cruelty to him, but didn't interrupt. I nodded.

"Even though all that bad stuff happened, it was okay. I knew it'd work out in the end," Muzo chirped.

I couldn't comprehend that. I was lucky to have never experienced such hardship, but when I put myself in his shoes, I felt nothing but dread. Where did one go when they had nothing?

"How?" I asked.

Muzo smiled up at me. "Because I'm still alive."

The strength of Muzo's resolve struck me like lightning. I was rooted to the spot, captivated endlessly by him.

"And if I'm alive, anything's possible," Muzo added. "Right?"

A shiver of emotion ran through me. This small, goofy omega was wiser than anybody gave him credit for.

"Right," I said slowly. Turning back to the tank, I asked, "Where have you seen this before?"

Muzo suddenly chuckled. "Oh, yeah, I forgot half my story. So, when I was a kid, I went on an awesome cruise with my mom. My dad was never in the picture, so it was just the two of us. Anyway, it was our first vacation ever.

She'd saved up for a year at her cashier job. I was freaking stoked!"

I smiled along with his enthusiasm.

"So we bought our tickets and showed up to board. That's when we saw the 'no shifters' sign." Muzo's grin lost its luster. "My mom checked the tickets, and sure enough, it was in the fine print, too. She'd been so excited to take me on a vacation that she didn't check thoroughly."

A cold feeling settled in my stomach like silt.

"But it was fine," Muzo went on. "She told me to stay in my human form, and everything would be okay. I could totally do that, so aboard we went!"

Sensing the story was about to take a turn for the worst, I subconsciously moved closer to him.

"We had an awesome time," Muzo said. "It was so much fun running around on a big ship, seeing the ocean, and eating as much shrimp as I wanted."

I made a mental note to provide shrimp for him at the next opportunity.

"Anyways, it was a family cruise, so there were a bunch of other kids my age on board. We ran around chasing each other while our parents chilled." Muzo paused thoughtfully. "And probably had a little too much to drink, now that I think about it, 'cause nobody was chaperoning us."

The unsettled feeling flared up again. I put my hand on Muzo's shoulder as a reminder that it was in the past, and that he was safe. Whether the reminder was for his sake or mine, I didn't know.

Muzo continued. "At one point, I got tired, so I took a break to look at the ocean. I leaned against the railing. My palms were all sweaty from chasing and being chased. But the other kids were still full of energy. They roughhoused

138

as one big pack of unsupervised children... and they knocked me overboard."

I held my breath. It was in the past, and Muzo was here with me now, but that didn't stop the chill in my blood.

Muzo was quiet for a moment as he stared into the tank. "I shifted out of instinct. The second I hit the water, I was in jackal form, doggy paddling for my life. I heard later that on the ship, nobody knew what to do. They all stared at me in disbelief 'cause they thought I was human, just like them. I wasn't even supposed to be there."

I kept waiting for the crack of emotion in Muzo's voice, but it never came. He didn't seem hurt when he had every right to be. How could so much positivity fit in one tiny omega?

"What happened next?" I asked.

Muzo tilted his head. "After a while, my legs got tired. I stopped struggling. I didn't know when—or if—help was coming, so I figured I'd save my energy. For a minute, I sank below the surface and closed my eyes..." He pressed a hand to the glass. "And I saw this place."

A chill ran down my spine.

"What?" I breathed.

"I dunno if it was a hallucination or vision or what, but it looked exactly like this room," Muzo murmured. "There was this big glass tank full of water and the snail and those silvery fish and these little shrimp. It was mostly empty, like yours is." Muzo angled his head towards me. "At the time, I really felt like I was *there*. Here, I mean. It was so peaceful and safe, I forgot I'd fallen overboard. I calmed down and shifted back. When I went up again for air, I was in human form, and the ship's crew sent down an emergency ladder for me."

Overwhelmed, I pulled Muzo into an embrace. He was

so much smaller than me that I had to lean down to bury my face in his hair. It smelled amazing. So *him*. I filled my lungs with his scent, content knowing he was here with me right now, safe and secure.

"I'm sorry that happened to you," I murmured.

Muzo laughed softly. "I appreciate that. But honestly, I'm glad it happened."

I frowned. "How can you be glad that humans pushed you overboard? You could've died."

"But I didn't. Besides, it was an accident. No harm, no foul." His smile reached his eyes. "If that never happened, I never would've seen that vision." He paused, a blush staining his cheeks. "I think it led me to you, Cobalt."

My heart squeezed with affection.

It was time to tell him.

"Muzo," I murmured. "I—"

He gasped, loud and sudden, as if hit by a revelation. He sputtered and pointed over my shoulder with unbridled enthusiasm. "Cobalt!"

"Huh?"

"The snail! There's another one!" Muzo cried.

I released him as he wriggled out of the hug and ran over to a different section of the tank. He glanced down at the snail in his bucket, then at the snail inside the aquarium.

"It's the same kind," Muzo exclaimed. "Did you know?"

I let out an amused huff as I joined him. "Are you asking if I know exactly what lives in my hoard?"

Muzo looked sheepish. "Oh, yeah. I guess that's a dumb question to ask a dragon."

I smiled, putting my hand on his shoulder. "I was only teasing. You're right. It's a Chromatimaeus brackish river snail—the same one as in your bucket."

"Chromatimaeus brackish river snail," Muzo repeated, slow and deliberate. "Try saying *that* ten times fast... So wait, what exactly is your hoard, Cobalt? Is it everything in this room?"

"Not quite. It's difficult to describe." I nodded towards the nondescript brown and gray snail inside the tank. "My hoard is this specific creature's natural environment. A miniature ecosystem, you could say. A brackish river on our home island, complete with the same substrate, the same plants and animals. I've done my best to recreate it and make the most comfortable home possible."

Muzo cocked his head curiously. "Hold on. This whole gigantic chamber... is for a single little snail?"

I rubbed the back of my neck in embarrassment. "It's not flashy, or interesting to most people. But it's my passion."

"Cobalt," Muzo murmured.

I turned my head to avoid his gaze. "I'm sorry if you expected a fascinating hoard."

Muzo's laugh was unexpectedly warm. "What? No way, dude. This is *so* you!"

I blinked, looking back at him in confusion. "It is?"

"Cobalt, nobody else in the world is as kind as you. You went out of your way to make a super comfortable home for a plain little creature." Muzo blushed. "Kinda like what you did for me."

My alpha instincts blazed. "You are not plain. You're special to me, Muzo," I growled.

He grinned. "Just like the snail, right?"

I huffed, crossing my arms. "You're even more special to me than the snail. But yes, I understand your point."

Muzo glanced into the bucket. "Hey, you think this tank has enough space for two? I bet that guy would like a friend."

Hope blossomed within me. The snail *needed* a friend—a mate.

"It's interesting you say that. My original goal was to breed the snail and reintroduce them back to their natural habitat," I explained. "But this isn't an asexual species. I needed two snails, but for ages, I only had one. A single, lonely snail." I smiled at Muzo. "Not anymore. Thanks to you, the species has a fighting chance."

Muzo beamed with pure happiness. "Wow. That's the most romantic thing anyone's ever said to me."

As soon as the words left his mouth, he realized what he'd said. His cheeks flushed a deep color and he stammered, "I mean, I don't mean like—well, I did, but—"

I leaned down and captured his lips in a kiss.

Muzo let out a tiny squeak of surprise before giving in to it. He sighed, kissing me back. I wrapped my arms around his small back, holding him close.

It was a soft, innocent kiss—despite my dragon raging below the surface, demanding I kiss him harder, claim him, finally make him mine.

We pulled apart, breathless. Muzo's eyes gleamed with affection.

"You're mine," I said.

The words slipped out of me before I realized what was happening.

Muzo let out a dazed, airy laugh. "I am?"

My fingers dug into him. Not painful, but possessive.

"You're my fated mate, Muzo," I growled gently.

He stared at me. It didn't look like he was even breathing. Was it this much of a shock to him?

"I felt your trials among the humans as a pain in my heart," I went on. "It didn't subside until I found you. Until I knew you were safe."

Finally, Muzo blinked like he'd returned to his body. A

slow grin curved his mouth. "Until you ripped the door off its hinges, you mean."

I chuckled. "You could say that."

Muzo's cheeks flushed. He couldn't contain the joy bubbling inside him. "Fated mate, huh? Maybe I'm denser than an aquarium rock, but I had no idea."

Now that the truth was out in the open, I felt a cloud-soft lightness in my chest.

"The broken door on the first day didn't clue you in?" I asked.

"I figured it was an accident..."

"The overly indulgent gift basket wasn't a clue?"

"I just thought you were being nice!"

"And the sex we had that night?" I prompted.

Muzo shrugged. "Hey, stuff like that happens all the time on reality TV shows."

I snorted in amusement, then brushed my nose against his forehead. "Now you have no excuse," I said, holding him closer. "And nowhere to run."

He grinned, a hint of his inner jackal flashing in his dark eyes. "Who's running?"

A surge of feeling welled up in my ribs. Muzo was here. He was mine.

He was finally, *finally* mine.

Now I wanted to show him exactly how much he meant to me.

The half-lidded, sensual look on Muzo's face told me he wanted that, too. Fire ignited below my belly. I didn't care if the Games weren't over yet. My fated mate was right in front of me, and I wasn't going to waste a single moment with him.

Hungry with desire, I closed the space between our bodies—or at least, I tried to.

I'd forgotten Muzo was still holding the bucket.

"Oh," I said, glancing down at the beautiful, slimy creature. I looked up at Muzo bashfully. "We should take care of this first. Let me put the snail into the tank before we have sex."

Muzo cackled, nearly doubling over with laughter. He wiped a tear from his eye. "Okay, I take it back. *That* is now officially the most romantic thing anyone's ever said to me."

SEVENTEEN

Muzo

I'D NEVER BEEN anyone's fated mate before. But if the way Cobalt literally swept me off my feet and carried me into bed was any indication, I could definitely get used to it.

After the snails were united in the tank, Cobalt took me back into the bedroom. Outside, the sun was setting over the ocean, painting the room in pastel shades of pink and orange.

My heart raced as I lay in Cobalt's bed. It smelled like him—musky and calming with a hint of spice. I could've been wrapped up in his sheets forever if it meant never leaving the cocoon of his scent.

He hovered over me, his arms and legs on either side of my body. The glossy sheen in his eyes reminded me of his dragon form, and they seemed so vast, like the ocean's unfathomable depths.

I grasped the sides of his face. His rugged jaw was lined with pinpricks of stubble that felt pleasant against my hands.

He took one of my hands, then pressed a kiss to my palm that electrified my blood.

I inhaled a shaky breath. We'd been intimate before, but this felt different. Cobalt's presence seemed bigger this time. He felt hungrier. Primal.

Cobalt's lips parted. Instead of normal human teeth, I saw elongated dragon fangs. They grazed the sensitive plane of my palm, making my skin tingle. Within seconds, my blood buzzed, ringing in my ears.

He wasn't holding back anymore.

"That tickles," I said with a breathy giggle as his fangs brushed my skin.

I saw an amused glint in Cobalt's eyes. He wasn't overly expressive, but I liked that about him. He was the calm to my storm. I was loud and wore my heart on my sleeve; Cobalt was soft-spoken and kept his feelings close to his chest. He offered me the space to feel loudly and freely. His subtle smiles and soft laughs always felt like a gift because I knew they were genuine every time.

Cobalt's hands drifted over my shirt. He slipped it over my head, exposing my bare chest. I'd always felt kind of embarrassed by my scrawniness. Sure, I was an omega, but I was a small omega. I was never anyone's first choice.

Until now.

Cobalt stared at me like I was a raw steak and he was a wolf who hadn't eaten in weeks. I swear I saw drool trickling from the corners of his mouth. Seeing that wild, lusty expression on his usually stoic face was so hot.

"I want to claim you," Cobalt growled. His dragon's deep, gravelly voice slipped in, making me shiver with anticipation.

I grinned. Even now, he managed to be sweeter than pie. I was half-naked, pinned underneath him on his bed, and he *still* asked for permission.

"I ain't going anywhere," I promised. "Go ahead and claim me."

It was like a dam broke. Cobalt moved so fast I barely had time to process it. His mouth latched onto my shoulder while his hand cupped my cock through my jeans. I gasped. My heart raced faster than a jackrabbit.

This version of Cobalt was different than the one who gave me a hand job in my hotel room. He had an aura of danger, yet I still felt completely safe. I knew he'd never hurt me, but the wilder side of him was a total turn-on.

I moaned as Cobalt rubbed my trapped cock. His thumb grazed it in rough circles that sent jagged bolts of pleasure up my spine. I arched into it, chasing the sensation. Soon I was hard enough to ache.

"Pants," I groaned. My brain was scrambled. "Disappear them."

A low chuckle from Cobalt, then he deftly undid the button and zipper of my jeans, thrusting them down to my ankles. I shuddered as the cool air touched my heated skin, then cried out as Cobalt's eager hand returned to its post. It felt a thousand times better without the thick fabric in the way. Even through my underwear, it was heavenly.

Speaking of thick, my eyes widened when I felt Cobalt's erection brush against my leg. How could it possibly seem *bigger* than the first time?

"You're slick already," Cobalt said roughly in my ear.

Heat erupted in my cheeks. "How'd you know that?" I squeaked.

"I smell you."

His voice was quiet and guttural, possessive and primal. Just like with his hoard, I was seeing a private side of him nobody else was allowed to witness. Only me.

I'd never felt so special.

"Well, it's 'cause you went and turned me on so badly," I teased. "Sorry if I drench your sheets, but it's your fault."

Cobalt huffed in amusement. His lips—and fangs—grazed the shell of my ear.

In a soft voice, he ordered, "Drench them."

Well, shit. That was one way to turn a guy on.

My cock throbbed against its fabric cage, which was now wet with so much slick fluid that it had as much structural integrity as a damp piece of paper. I was about to ask Cobalt to take them off when he raised a hand, shifted his nails into dragon claws, then sliced them clean off.

"Hey, those could've been my lucky underpants," I protested jokingly.

Cobalt paused, leveling a serious look at me. "Were they?" he asked, actually worried.

I planted a reassuring kiss on his cheek. "No, but thanks for your concern."

Cobalt sighed in relief. "I'll buy you thirty more pairs of lucky underwear," he promised before capturing my lips.

I quickly dissolved into nothing but moans as Cobalt's tongue tangled with mine. With his big hand wrapped around my sensitive cock and his mouth claiming me, my entire body was alight with pleasure. I was taut as a pressurized spring, greedy for release, ready to explode.

But I didn't want this to end. Nobody had ever wanted me as desperately and passionately as Cobalt did. His desire for me was intoxicating.

Was this what being fated mates felt like? No wonder everybody wanted to find theirs so badly.

Our need for air finally broke our kiss apart. Cobalt panted heavily above me. His eyes blazed with lust. They looked draconic again, wild and ringed with spirals of neon blue. He was breathtakingly beautiful.

Man, being craved by an alpha dragon felt pretty damn good.

Cobalt dug his fingers into my arms. "Muzo," he murmured thickly. He sounded like he was barely hanging onto his sanity. "I need to breed you."

Tingles sparked across my skin.

Cobalt wanted to breed me.

My fated mate wanted to *impregnate* me.

"Yeah," I blurted without a second thought. Then I blushed because that was so not a romantic way to respond to Cobalt's sexy comment. "I mean, yes, please do that."

Cobalt smiled in the sweet way he always did when I stumbled over my words, since I was apparently really good at that.

His next words held a twinge of hesitation. "I can restrain myself. We don't need to rush. But if you want a family—"

"I do," I interrupted.

I stared him dead in the eyes. If his gaze looked intense a second ago, mine must've looked the same way now.

"I know I joke around and stuff, but this is what I've always wanted," I promised. "A mate. Kids. A family. I just never thought it'd happen so soon. Or even at all. I mean, that's why I entered the Dragonfate Games. Even if Taylor thought I was doing it to troll him."

Cobalt flashed a playful smirk. "I thought you came on for the free vacations."

"Okay, those were a nice bonus," I agreed. "But I obviously didn't gel with your brothers, so I had to keep coming back, right?"

A spark of possessiveness flashed across Cobalt's face, which was adorable since I literally just told him I wasn't interested in the other alphas. I laughed and patted his cheeks.

"You're so cute when you wanna rip your little brothers' heads off," I teased.

He sighed, calming down. "Dragon instincts. I'll keep them under control."

I paused, then wriggled my eyebrows. "What if I don't want you to?"

"How so?"

I glanced down at the monster cock bulging out of his trousers, then pointedly back at him. "All I'm saying is, if you wanna be a freak in the privacy of the bedroom..."

A slow, hungry grin spread over Cobalt's face. He rose up and tossed off his shirt, followed promptly by his pants and briefs.

My eyes must've bulged out of my face when I saw his massive cock because *wow*.

"Did you take enhancement pills or something since the last time?" I asked.

"No," Cobalt said simply. "It's because of my attraction to you."

I didn't know if he was joking or if it was a dragon thing or what, but I stopped thinking about it.

"That," I said, pointing at it, "is not gonna fit."

Cobalt pouted, his excited expression faltering. "I was afraid of that..."

I suddenly felt bad. I shook my head. "No, it's fine. We'll make it work. We're fated mates, right? Fate wouldn't give you a dick that won't fit in my ass."

A chuckle escaped Cobalt. "Now who's the one being romantic?"

"I try. Let's see..."

First things first, all remaining clothes had to go. I tossed them on the floor.

Next came the challenge of actually fitting that behemoth inside me.

I kneeled on the bed in front of Cobalt's cock. As I

watched it twitch, I gulped in anticipation. It was like a creature all its own, standing proudly before me.

I tentatively ran my hands down its sides. Cobalt groaned. His deep dragon's voice mixed with his own, making a perfectly sultry sound that went straight to my balls.

I shuffled closer to the towering giant, aligning it with my body. I choked in disbelief as the length of Cobalt's erection spanned from the base of my thighs to the bottom of my rib cage.

Cobalt blushed. "I'm sorry."

I snorted. "What're you sorry for? I love you and your body. Every part of it."

His blush turned a deeper color. "You love me?"

"Well, yeah!" I blurted. "You're the one who said we're fated mates. Isn't that obvious?"

Cobalt smiled, leaning forward to kiss my cheek. "Yes. I love you, too."

A million butterflies fluttered in my chest. Damn, it felt nice to hear those words.

"As much as I love being sappy, let's get your dick in me first," I said.

A lust-rough chuckle escaped him. "Good idea."

I figured we could try the old-fashioned way first. Lying back on the bed, I nodded at Cobalt. He slowly aligned the tip of his cock with my entrance. I hissed in pleasure as it rubbed against my slick hole.

My body definitely wanted him. Actually *taking* him was a different story.

"Are you ready?" he asked.

I gave him a thumbs up. "Go for it."

The thumbs up quickly turned into a desperate grapple for the sheets as Cobalt entered me. Sweat prickled my skin. I gasped as the hot, tight sensation spread.

"Phew," I said, already breathless.

Cobalt stopped moving. "Are you all right?"

I nodded slowly as my body adjusted to the intrusion. "Yeah. Go on."

Cobalt gently eased in deeper. The feeling was strange, but oh so good. Pleasure sizzled across my body, smothering the discomfort from being stretched to my limit.

I lay there relaxing my muscles for what felt like an eternity. Surely Cobalt was all the way in by now...

I raised my head to check the situation down there. "How deep?" I asked.

"Two inches. Maybe three," Cobalt replied.

"Three?" I cried. "That's it? It feels like the Empire State Building's shoved up there!"

"The what?"

"Never mind."

I flopped back on the bed, disappointed with myself. Why couldn't I take more of Cobalt?

C'mon, ass! Try harder!

Cobalt's soft voice broke into my thoughts. "Muzo. I don't *have* to fit all the way inside to breed you."

I lifted my head to meet his gaze.

"That's true," I mumbled.

"It's not a personal failing," he reassured, as if reading my mind. "We can always try to work up to it. We have time."

My heart squeezed with love. Why was he the nicest, sweetest alpha in the history of ever?

"Yeah, you're right," I conceded.

He leaned over to kiss me. It felt doubly good with the head of his cock still buried inside me. I moaned into his mouth as our tongues melted together. Everything felt so wet and hot and *amazing*.

A sudden movement down below made me gasp. Our

kiss had loosened my muscles and let Cobalt's dick slip in deeper.

"Keep doing that," I demanded.

Cobalt huffed through a smirk. "I don't need orders for that."

He kissed me harder, deeper—matching the pace of his cock within me. As Cobalt's tongue twisted around mine, his throbbing length inched further in. I thought I'd been stretched to my limit before, but that was nothing compared to the thick sensation now.

Finally, I hit my limit.

"Fuck," I whimpered against his mouth. "Can't take anymore."

Cobalt nodded and pressed a kiss to my forehead. "Okay."

He glanced down, as if making a mental note of where my limit was in relation to his dick, then smoothed his warm hands across my chest. I relaxed under his touch, sighing in happiness. Every little thing he did made me feel wanted and loved.

"By the way," I said. "I don't care if it doesn't fit all the way. I still don't want you to hold back your dragon side."

Cobalt's eyes flashed, almost glowing in the darkness. The sunset colors in the room had gone from pink to dusky purple, bathing the room in twilight shadows.

"Are you sure?" he asked in a low voice.

"As long as you don't rip me in two, go for it."

A growl vibrated in Cobalt's throat. "I would never hurt my mate."

I grinned. "I know, Cobalt. I'm only joking."

Cobalt frowned. "But... I do want to bite you."

An unexpected flicker of pleasure ran through me. "You do?"

He grimaced like he was battling his instinctive urges.

"My dragon wants to claim you. In every possible way. Biting is one of those ways."

He sounded guilty for some reason, as if that wasn't sexy as fuck.

"Then bite me," I said. "Gimme the whole dragon breeding experience, please. And don't worry about hurting me. I know my limits. If it gets too bad, I'll tap out." I smiled. "Trust me, okay?"

He exhaled through his nose. "Okay."

Cobalt closed his eyes and breathed. When he opened them, the neon rings in his eyes pulsated like circles of blue fire.

Then his nails elongated into dragon talons. Leathery wings snapped out of his back. His hair grew longer and shaggier, resembling his dragon's mane. When his mouth parted to breathe heavily, I saw his glinting fangs.

My eyes widened. I couldn't breathe.

Half-shifted in front of me, Cobalt was the hottest thing I'd ever seen.

Cobalt arched his body over me like a predator. His ragged breath ghosted across my skin in hot puffs. His claws sank into the bed on either side of me, not caring that he tore the expensive sheets to shreds. His primal gaze bore into me, needy and hungry.

My cock was so freaking hard, I couldn't stand it.

As his dragon side took over, Cobalt started fucking me. I choked on a pleasured cry. I threw my head back into the pillow as electric jolts skated over my nerves.

"Fuck," I cried. "Fuck, Cobalt, that feels good..."

A loud growl echoed in the room. I was a prey animal trapped in the dragon's lair. The edge of danger only turned me on more. I knew Cobalt wouldn't actually hurt me, so it was fun to pretend.

My mind went blank as Cobalt's thrusts picked up

speed. The friction of his thick cock plowing in and out of my sensitive hole drove me crazy. I moaned and whimpered and made a bunch of other sounds I didn't remember. All I could focus on was the hot pleasure scorching my body.

Cobalt suddenly lunged for me. His fangs sank into the space where my neck met my shoulder. There was pain for a second, like the brief sting of a needle, but it instantly dissolved into ecstasy. I writhed as it swept over me in a monsoon of pleasure.

Cobalt's tongue licked over the wounds. It felt like the bite was over too soon. Was it weird that I wanted more?

When Cobalt pulled back, his eyes leaned human instead of dragon. "Are you all right?" he murmured.

I grabbed the back of his neck. My fingers tangled through his long, messy mane.

"I might just come if you bite me like that again," I said breathlessly.

The rings flared in Cobalt's eyes as they shifted back to dragon.

Cobalt lunged again. As his fangs sank into my skin, my cock strained against my belly. Suddenly, he grabbed my wrists and hiked them above my head. Cobalt drew back from the bite, giving my skin a tender lick, then dove into my armpit.

"Ah!" I squeaked. "W-wait, I haven't showered yet—"

"Don't care," Cobalt snarled.

His wet tongue glided across my armpit, making me writhe.

The sudden deluge of pleasure was a shock to my system. Heat streaked across my skin. My mind whited out. The wet, dominant sensation of Cobalt's tongue turned me brainless. It should've felt so wrong, but it was so right.

As Cobalt licked my armpit, he huffed my scent

hungrily, like a wolf drooling over raw steak. It flustered me to see him act so feral. It was the polar opposite of his usual dignified self, but this was part of him, too—a side that nobody else had ever witnessed. Only me. That made his descent into lust-crazed madness even more special.

As my muscles relaxed, Cobalt's cock inched in deeper. Every time I felt like I was at my final limit, my alpha ignited a new burst of pleasure in me, loosening my body for him. Each twitch of his thick cock struck a nerve. I crackled, as sensitive as a live wire. My blood itself vibrated.

Cobalt finally drew away from my armpit. He was completely undone with desire. The whole bottom of his jaw was wet. He rolled his tongue over his sharp fangs before it lolled out of his mouth.

"Now," he said roughly. "The other."

Cobalt didn't hesitate. He dove into my other armpit with greedy fervor, attacking it with his tongue. I cried out, writhing against the bed. It didn't even tickle—it just felt so sensitive, and so weirdly *good*.

It was all too much. I was veering towards the edge too fast to stop.

"Can't take it," I breathed.

Cobalt gripped me harder. His talons dug into me, as did his thrusting cock.

"Come while I breed you," he growled.

Fireworks. Violent, fraying sparks of light.

That was all I saw behind my eyes as I came. I wasn't even aware of the hoarse sound tearing from my throat. I felt like I was in an entirely different world, one made purely of pleasure. In the fuzzy distance, I heard a climactic dragon's roar.

Other sensations slowly crept back into my conscious-ness. A familiar wetness on my lower belly—definitely my own fault. But there was another wetness, a thick flood of it in the deepest part of me.

The sudden realization made my head swim—I was full of Cobalt's seed. He bred me, just like he promised.

A weight shifted. My hole twitched and I shuddered as Cobalt gently eased his way out.

I blinked as I came back to reality. My mate was no longer on top, but curled next to me. I turned to face him. We were equally flushed and drenched in sweat.

"Hi," I said with a satisfied grin.

Cobalt's rugged mouth curled into a smile mirroring my own. "Hi."

Overcome with a rush of fondness, I shimmied closer to him, snuggling as close as physically possible. Cobalt wrapped his arms around my back. I sighed contentedly against his chest. I experienced the purest sense of safety and happiness as I lay there, warm and protected and totally surrounded by Cobalt.

Maybe... Just maybe...

Could Cobalt be my fated mate after all?

EIGHTEEN

Cobalt

A STERN KNOCK at the door rudely awakened me.

I let out a muffled groan and snuggled closer to Muzo. I didn't even bother opening my eyes. Whoever was at the door could wait. Morning cuddles with my mate were more important.

The knock came again. Louder.

Muzo yawned. "Who'sat?"

"Don't know. Don't care." I kissed his warm forehead. "Don't worry about it."

Muzo made a contented sound, burying himself in my arms. "'kay."

The insistent knock came a third time.

"Go away," I called.

The intruder fell silent. I sighed in relief, happy to be done with that. This early morning moment with my mate was precious. I didn't want anybody to interfere.

But when the knock came a fourth time, I grabbed Blueberry and threw him at the door so hard it caused a loud *thump*.

Muzo gasped. "Blueberry! You killed him!"

"He's full of stuffing. He's fine," I mumbled. "Go back to sleep."

"It's hard to sleep after witnessing plushie murder..."

I hauled myself out of bed, picked Blueberry off the floor, dusted him off, then plopped him back in Muzo's waiting arms. My mate lit up as he hugged the abused plushie to his chest.

"Yay! Now we can go back to sleep," he decided.

Just as I was about to crawl back into bed, the door clicked. I watched, flabbergasted, as it swung open to reveal Jade. He held up one finger, which sported a dragon claw at the end. He didn't look pleased to see me.

The feeling was mutual. "Since when do you know how to pick locks?" I grumbled.

Jade's claw shifted back and he crossed his arms. "I'm glad you asked. I read about it recently in one of the many books in my library, and this was a good opportunity to practice what I'd learned."

"Oh, hey, Jade!" Muzo called from the bed, waving.

Jade smiled at him. "Good morning, Muzo." The smile fell off his face when he turned back to me. "Do you have any idea what time it is?"

I hesitated.

Jade provided the answer for me. "No, you don't." He checked his silver watch. "It is now 10 AM. You were supposed to be on the beach an hour ago. I reassured every member of staff *and* the contestants you would be present. I assumed you would be there, given our talk about responsibility."

I grimaced as guilt slammed into me. Jade was right—again. When I agreed to be the bachelor of the Games, I took on certain duties. It embarrassed me that my younger brothers did a better job at this than I did.

"I'm sorry for skirting my responsibilities," I said. "But I'm not sorry for spending the night with Muzo."

"I didn't say you had to be," Jade pointed out.

"Oh, crap," Muzo said, sounding down. "Is this my fault?"

"No," I said instantly.

Jade nodded. "You're fine, Muzo. Cobalt is the one who whisked you away to the castle and ravaged you," he added with a smirk.

I shrugged. There was no point in denying it. If the two naked men caught in bed weren't enough of an indication, then the lingering scent of sex in the air was the nail in the coffin.

"I'm happy for you two, truly," Jade said, putting a hand on his chest. "Just try to remember that *someone* has to be in charge of running the Games, hm? And I can't run them if the big bad bachelor himself can't be bothered to show up."

I hung my head. "Yes. You're right."

Jade sighed. "It's fine. I should've seen this coming from a mile away since you barely paid attention during the challenge briefing."

"The what?"

"Do you even remember the concepts we discussed?"

I balked. "Um..."

"I rest my case," Jade said, amused despite himself. "At the time, you half-heartedly agreed to a quiz show about yourself, like Thystle did on his season. Although I doubt it would have been a success, given how little the contestants know you."

I rubbed my temple. "I don't even remember agreeing to that."

Back then, I was so distracted by Muzo's distant suffering that I couldn't think of anything else. All I knew was that my fated mate was out there somewhere, going through hardships. I was glad to finally have him in my arms where he could be safe forever.

"So, what are they doing instead?" I asked.

At some point, Muzo had climbed out of bed to peer out the window. Apparently after so many nudity-related incidents, he no longer had any qualms about it. He stood naked with Blueberry clutched to his chest as he overlooked the distant beach. "Looks like Gaius is doing some kinda dance," he told us. "Either that, or he's seizing."

When I raised a brow, Jade shrugged and said, "Somebody had to entertain people."

"He just took his shirt off!" Muzo called.

I pinched the bridge of my nose. I had to fix the situation before Gaius stripped on camera and scarred the contestants for life.

"Can't we just go out there and tell the truth?" I suggested.

Jade paused thoughtfully. "I'm listening."

"I'll tell the contestants exactly what happened. That I couldn't control my draconic urges, and I took Muzo to the castle because I knew he was my fated mate."

"It's true, he really couldn't control his urges," Muzo agreed.

Jade stroked his chin. "Actually, that's not a bad idea. I'm sure the audience would appreciate your honesty. And everybody *did* see you shift and steal Muzo away. We've got the whole thing on film."

I frowned at the villainous implication. "I didn't steal him. He wanted to come."

Muzo nodded. "Consent was involved!"

"Yes, that's all good," Jade said, sounding distracted. He was probably playing 3D chess in his mind as he tried to twist the situation to our advantage. "My point is, an alpha dragon's passion is a powerful tool in our kit. It might not matter to the audience that Cobalt found his mate instantly if we focus on your love instead." He snapped his fingers. "Muzo, throw on some clothes. Cobalt, bring him to the beach ASAP. Dragon form for added flair, please."

He turned on his heel to leave, then raised a finger.

"And if you're late this time, I'm going to slice up more than just a lock, if you catch my drift."

———

WE LANDED on the beach just as Gaius turned his bright pink button-up into a makeshift Hula skirt. He looked disappointed that we'd interrupted his drag show.

"Please put the shirt back on, Gaius," I ordered.

He grinned. "Cobalt! Nice to see you. Are you sure? We were just getting to the good part!"

I raised a scaly eyebrow at him.

He pouted and put the shirt on.

Once Gaius was fully dressed, he took back the mic. That spontaneous intermission would be cut out of the final aired footage, so he launched back into his hosting duties as if it never happened. Jade took Gaius aside and quickly filled him in on what was happening.

While they spoke, I gazed out at the gathered contestants. Most stared at us in awe. I recognized Poppy, who looked as happy as a kid on his birthday. Beside him, Alaric looked bored.

But other contestants looked visibly disappointed. They must've realized at this point there was no hope of finding their mate this season.

I felt a pang of sympathy for those omegas. I knew firsthand the loneliness that came from being mateless.

I placed Muzo on the sand between my front paws, then nuzzled his temple with the tip of my snout. He grinned and patted my scales.

Gaius strutted out in front of us, mic in hand. "Wow, talk about a turn of events! After our alpha dragon bachelor was late to the party, we all wondered where he could be."

I withheld a snort. I wondered if Jade made him say that as a light jab in my direction.

Gaius went on, gesturing to us in a sweeping motion. "But there's no mistaking that he's here with us now—with Muzo to boot! Can either of you two explain what exactly happened between yesterday and now?"

I'd been carefully preparing my words since Jade left this morning. I cleared my throat. "Well, Gaius—"

"We had sex," Muzo declared happily.

Silence fell over the beach. Even Gaius was at a loss for words for a moment.

"Well, no one can say you aren't honest," he continued with a laugh. The easygoing way he went with the flow eased the crowd, as if his good mood allowed them to relax. "Cobalt, can you confirm or deny this statement?"

I mentally threw my speech out the window. There was no going back now.

I swept my long tail around Muzo. He giggled as the furry tip tickled him.

"I confirm it wholeheartedly," I answered.

The camera crew edged closer from every angle, eagerly capturing shots of us together. Jade stood by them with a satisfied expression. Being late was a blessing in disguise. Rare footage of my dragon form combined with the unprecedented interruption to the Games must be a goldmine for a reality TV show.

At the back of the crowd, Jade made a subtle 'go on' hand gesture.

I cleared my throat. "I want to apologize to the other contestants that I missed the challenge. The fault is all mine. But I'll be honest. The allure of my fated mate was too much to bear. I couldn't be apart from him a second longer."

The second I dropped the words 'fated mate,' the contestants broke into a clamor. It took Gaius a minute to quiet everyone down. I noticed Poppy and Alaric didn't join in. Had they already suspected something?

"Does that mean the Dragonfate Games are already over?" an apprehensive omega asked Gaius.

"That's not fair," an angrier one butted in. "They barely started! How can Cobalt possibly know who his mate is?"

Fire sizzled in my heart. When I spoke, my dragon's voice boomed, capturing everyone's attention in an instant.

"Do not doubt fate," I growled. "The legendary bond between an alpha and omega fated to be together is something that cannot be faked. I *know* Muzo is my mate. That is final."

The crowd went dead silent.

Oops. I'd forgotten I was in my dragon form—and thus, every word out of my mouth was terrifying. I hoped my speech didn't frighten the rest of the contestants.

Thankfully, Gaius dispelled the tension just by being himself. He clapped enthusiastically like I'd given a rehearsed performance. "Beautiful words from our alpha dragon bachelor. Although it seems he's not quite a bachelor anymore!" He wagged a finger. "But not to worry, contestants. The Dragonfate Games aren't quite over yet. In our third and final challenge, you won't be fighting for the dragon's affections."

Gaius paused purposefully, letting the anticipation sink in. The crowd murmured in confusion. Hell, I was confused, too. What would they compete for in his place?

Gaius finally broke his silence. "Instead, you'll have the chance to win a cash prize of one million dollars!"

The contestants erupted into ecstatic, frenzied chaos. It was almost comical. Compared to a million bucks, I was nothing. They acted like I didn't even exist anymore.

That was fine by me. This was a win-win situation for everybody.

Except my wallet.

Jade instructed the contestants to return to the hotel to prepare for the final challenge. After the contestants left, I remained on the beach with Muzo, Gaius, Jade and some straggling staff members. One of them handed me a spare outfit after I shifted back to human form.

"One million?" I asked Jade, raising a brow.

He shamelessly arched a brow right back at me. "You got yourself into this mess, Cobalt. Now you're getting yourself out of it."

"Sure. But you couldn't have settled for five hundred thousand?"

"I'm charging you extra for emotional damages," he said wryly.

I sighed. "Fair enough."

Gaius ignored our brotherly spat. "Aren't you two a sight for sore eyes," he said, grinning at me and Muzo. "Look what a cute couple you are! Your size difference is to die for."

Out of nowhere, a pair of golden dragons swooped in, shifted in mid-air, then landed on the sand next to us. The remaining staff had already left so there was nobody around to save our eyes from the twins' casual nudity.

"Yeah, it's like the difference between a Great Dane and a Chihuahua," Aurum said with a snort.

"Hey, they can still breed, y'know," Saffron pointed out.

Cutting off their conversation before it devolved into obscenity, I asked, "What are you two doing here?"

"Snooping," Aurum admitted. "Jade said we're not allowed to be on set during filming. Because of the 'sanctity of the Games,'" he added with heavy air quotes and a roll of his eyes. He thrust a thumb at Jade. "But he is, for some reason?"

Jade smiled primly. "I'm different. Also, I don't wear disguises and leak information to contestants, like I recall a certain pair of dragons doing last season."

Aurum stuck his tongue out at Jade. Meanwhile, his twin was busy making googly eyes at us.

"I can't believe you guys disrupted the Games and caused such a big scene." Saffron said it like it was a good thing. He sighed, clasping his hands together. "It was so romantic."

Muzo grinned, nodding along with him. "It really was, wasn't it?"

Aurum made a silent gagging gesture.

"It was reckless," Jade corrected mildly. "But it all worked out in the end."

"Sorry for the trouble," I said.

Jade smirked. "It's all right. You're paying for your crime. Literally."

He looked way too pleased with himself for that dig.

"But if this is going to be an ongoing trend, perhaps I need to do some thinking about the next season," Jade murmured, shooting a strange look at Aurum.

My golden-haired brother didn't notice. He was too busy prying Saffron away from Muzo.

"Cut it out, bro," Aurum said. "The guy almost drowned once already, he doesn't need you *gushing* over him."

"I'm okay with gushing," Muzo said with a nod. He gasped suddenly. "I just realized something. If me and Cobalt are fated mates, does that mean we're all family now?"

"Dude!" Saffron said excitedly.

Muzo grabbed his hands. "*Dude.*"

Aurum groaned loudly, turning to Gaius. "Give me your pink shirt. I need something to hurl into."

As usual, Gaius was completely unfazed. "You'll never snag yourself an omega with an attitude like that, young man," he said chipperly, patting Aurum on the back.

Aurum slunk out of his reach. "Welp, I'm going home before I die from cringe. You coming, bro?"

There were technically three brothers present he could've been referring to, but we all knew he meant his twin.

"In a sec," Saffron said. "I wanna talk to Muzo."

The mix of annoyance and heartbreak on Aurum's face was almost painful to look at. Without another word, he shifted aggressively and flew off. What was worse was that Saffron didn't even seem to notice.

I frowned, worried about my younger brothers' ongoing tiff, but Muzo's tug on my arm caught my attention.

"Hey, I know we spent all last night and this morning together, but..." He grinned shyly. "Is it okay if we go back to your room again tonight?"

Warmth bloomed in my chest. I loved knowing he wanted to spend as much time with me as I did with him.

I smiled, pulling him into my grasp. "You don't even have to ask."

NINETEEN

Muzo

I SAT on the edge of Cobalt's bed, kicking my legs impatiently. After the third challenge was postponed, he took me back to the castle just like I'd asked.

Correction: he took me back *home.*

A tingly mix of hope and relief filled my chest. I flopped down on the bed with a content sigh.

This still didn't feel real. Everything happened so fast. I expected the third season of the Dragonfate Games to be like the first two—fun, but ultimately, I'd go home alone.

Not this time.

It wasn't because I no longer had a home to go back to but because *this* was my home now.

And Cobalt—the biggest, eldest, most adorably sweet dragon alpha—was my fated mate.

I grinned like an idiot. Just thinking about him made my heart skate around in circles. I loved him so much.

So, where the hell was he?

I sat upright on the bed and stared at the door harder, as if that'd make him manifest. Once we returned to his room, he told me to wait here for a few minutes, then he skedaddled. It was the first time we'd been separated since before the second challenge yesterday, and it felt weird. I liked being by his side.

I sighed, grabbed Blueberry to my chest, and limply fell onto the bed again. As cute as the plushie was, he was a poor substitute for my *real* giant squishy marshmallow alpha.

When the door opened, I bolted upright in excitement. It was only slightly dulled by seeing a different dragon, but I was happy all the same.

"Oh, hey Saffron," I greeted.

The blond twin scampered into the room and leapt on the bed beside me. We'd become fast friends since the snooping session on the beach. Unlike his twin, Saffron was keenly interested in my relationship with Cobalt.

Saffron grinned, lounging on the bed like he belonged there. "Hey, Muzo."

"Do you know where Cobalt is? He told me to stay put, then wandered off," I said with a pout.

Saffron snorted with laughter. "He's in Crimson's room getting schooled by the fashion police."

"Why?"

"Guess when he wanted advice, he went crawling back to Crimson after all." Saffron nodded at the blue dragon clutched in my arms. "Hey, you really like that plushie, huh?"

"I don't like him. I *love* him." I rubbed my cheek against Blueberry's face. "Before I knew I was staying here on the island, I seriously considered abandoning half my wardrobe so I could take him back with me."

Saffron took out his phone and typed something quickly.

"What'cha doing?" I asked.

"Taking notes," he answered, pocketing the phone.

"For what?"

"How to be a good alpha."

I tilted my head. "Huh. I thought that came naturally."

Saffron shrugged. "I want to be prepared for my turn. I don't want to blow it because I don't know how to act." He poked Blueberry's chest, then asked, "Do you think I could commission Taylor to make one of these for me, too?"

I grinned. "I'm sure he'd love any excuse to show off his awesome sewing skills."

Saffron perked up, encouraged at the idea. "Okay, cool. I'm gonna tell him to make it twice as big. No, three times."

A familiar dry voice came from the door. "What kind of abomination am I being forced to create?" Taylor asked.

I gasped. "Tay!"

I flew off the bed faster than lightning and launched myself at him in a big hug.

"Oof." Taylor patted my back. "Hey, Muzo."

"I missed you so much," I said, though it came out muffled against his shirt.

Taylor smiled. "I missed you, too. Even though it's only been a few months since the last Games."

"Yeah, but it's been different back in the city since you moved away. Just me and Poppy against the world."

Taylor sounded amused. "You make it sound like you're a pair of sad abandoned puppies instead of two grown men."

"I *felt* like a sad abandoned puppy."

Taylor gave me another solid pat. "Saffron, do yourself a favor and hope for a feline fated mate. Canines are clingy by nature. Exhibit A is currently stuck to my shirt."

Saffron's phone keyboard clicked as he wrote that down. "Noted. By the way, where's Ruby?"

"Viol is babysitting," Taylor explained. "When

Crimson heard that Cobalt actually *wanted* his help getting dressed for once, he dropped everything, including parenting responsibilities."

Saffron cackled. "Father of the Year award over there."

"He'll make up for it. Despite his quirks, he's an incredible father," Taylor said warmly.

Since he found his fated mate in Crimson, Taylor had softened around the edges. He was still the serious, sassy tiger I always knew, but his love for Crimson and Ruby shone through his every word.

Saffron shuddered. "Man, I still can't believe you let that personified rusty switchblade watch your kid. You should pick more responsible babysitters. Like me and Aurum."

Taylor arched a brow. "*You*, maybe. I wouldn't trust Aurum to babysit a pet rock."

"Hey, he's not that bad," Saffron said, though he didn't sound convinced, either.

After a pause, Taylor said, "You two have been arguing a lot recently. Is everything all right?"

"Yeah, it's cool," Saffron mumbled, grabbing Blueberry. "Yo, Taylor, can you make me one of these, too? But bigger? And make it look like *my* dragon instead?"

Taylor must've figured Saffron didn't want to continue that conversation, so he nodded. "Sure. I expect full payment upfront. And since it'll be three times bigger, expect to pay three times as much."

"Aw, man," Saffron muttered, sitting upright and looking around the room. "Where's Cobalt's wallet?"

The victim of the almost-theft responded: "In my pocket, where it belongs."

I grinned excitedly at the sound of Cobalt's voice. Tearing myself away from Taylor, I latched onto my mate instead. Hugging my friend was nice, but hugging Cobalt was special. He was huge and soft and warm and he smelled so freaking *good*.

After getting my necessary hug out of the way, I noticed Cobalt's fancy outfit. He wore a perfectly fitted blue suit that complemented his hair and eyes. His crisp white shirt and shoes gave him a mature, wealthy aura.

"Whoa." I whistled, looking him up and down. "Hello, handsome."

A light blush dusted Cobalt's pale cheeks. He put his hands on my waist. "You look handsome as always, too."

"Well?" Crimson said by way of greeting as he strode proudly into the room. "Did I outdo myself or what? Our dear older brother looks like he belongs on the cover of a magazine, doesn't he?"

Taylor smirked. "Of course you put him in a suit."

Crimson scoffed in mock offence, but he was clearly amused, too. "Get your mind out of the gutter, kitten."

The two mates exchanged a mysterious, knowing look. I figured it was an inside joke or something.

Cobalt cleared his throat and handed me a folded card. "Here. Open it."

"Ooh, another card," I said. When I flipped it open, I smiled at Cobalt's familiar clunky handwriting.

> *DEAR MUZO,*
> *I OWE YOU A DINNER DATE*
> *MEET ME AT THE ROOF AT SUNSET*
> *YOUR FATED MATE,*
> *COBALT*

A wave of emotion hit me. I threw myself at Cobalt for another embrace.

"Well? Do you accept my invitation?" he asked, like it was even a question.

I chuckled, remembering what he said to me before. "You don't even have to ask."

THE VIEW from the castle rooftop was beautiful—sky, forest, and ocean as far as the eye could see. Chromatimaeus Island was truly its own little paradise.

And now, it was my home.

Cobalt had a candlelit table prepared for our arrival. Rose petals were scattered across the tablecloth. As we took our seats, a kobold server filled our glasses with water.

"I've gotta admit, this is a lot fancier than I'm used to," I said with a sheepish grin. "Hell, a few weeks ago, I was eating out of a Dumpster."

"You won't be doing that anymore," Cobalt promised.

There was a hint of his dragon's sexy growl in his tone. I squeezed my thighs together under the table. No getting worked up at the fancy dinner.

My nose suddenly caught a delicious whiff. I sat upright. A second later, the server returned with a sizzling plate of freshly grilled shrimp, placing it in the middle of the table.

I gasped. "Cobalt! How'd you know I love shrimp?"

"You mentioned it during your cruise story. I was happy it was something I could easily provide."

Practically drooling, I grabbed a fork and went to jab the nearest shrimp, then paused. "Wait, wait. These aren't the shrimp from your hoard, are they? I couldn't bear to eat those little guys."

He chuckled. "No, Muzo. Everything in my hoard is safe and sound."

"Okay, good," I said, then munched on the shrimp guilt-free. The smoky taste of the grill combined with the juicy shrimp meat almost made me moan. I went into a gluttonous shrimp frenzy, eating five more before I returned to my senses. "Damn. That beats leftover burger wrappers any day."

Cobalt reached across the table and placed his large, warm hand on top of mine. "Whatever you want, Muzo, it's yours. Let me take care of you. Let me make up for those weeks you spent hungry on the streets."

My heart squeezed. I never thought of myself as being *that* emotional, but since falling in love with Cobalt, I got slapped with feelings all the time. Cobalt's words were so kind and generous that I couldn't even think of a playful answer.

"I'd like that," I murmured with a soft smile.

Cobalt smiled back, mirroring my bliss. It made him happy to make me happy. I couldn't believe I was this damn lucky.

"Shall I call for a menu?" Cobalt asked.

I glanced hungrily down at the shrimp plate. "I'm gonna be real with you, Cobalt. I could eat this whole thing and be satisfied."

His blue eyes twinkled. "Just like you ate all that chocolate before our previous date?" he teased.

I let out a mix of a groan and a laugh. "I regretted it after, okay? I thought I had to eat it all while I could. I didn't know I'd win the Dragonfate Games for once and stay here forever."

"I know," he said gently. His fingers captured mine. "You're home now, Muzo."

Home. Here on Chromatimaeus Island.

It was a mouthful, but hey, it had a nice ring to it.

TWENTY

Cobalt

_____

AFTER OUR DINNER DATE, I imagined a cozy night of cuddling together in bed.

Instead, Muzo wanted to check on the snails. That worked just as well for me.

It still felt surreal that he showed as much interest in my hoard as I did, but I suppose that was to be expected of fated mates.

"I just wanna see how they're getting along," he said, running up to the glass. "Look, Cobalt!"

His enthusiasm lit up the room. Usually my hoard was a place of calm solitude, a place I went to be alone with my thoughts. The oddness of my collection kept me from sharing it with even my family. But sharing it with Muzo was wonderful. His honest curiosity and open zeal were refreshing.

It made me rethink keeping my hoard hidden. If he accepted it, could my brothers accept it, too?

I followed Muzo up to the glass. "What is it?" I asked.

He pointed to a rocky outcrop framed by two strands of kelp. I gasped. The two snails sat shell by shell in a picture-perfect scene.

"They're hanging out together," Muzo said. "Did you put them nearby on purpose, Cobalt?"

I shook my head. "In my research, they're known to be territorial, so when I placed the second snail in the tank, I gave them plenty of space so they could get used to each other slowly. But it appears they didn't need it."

"Aww. They're already best friends." He grinned. "Or maybe more?"

"Let's cross our fingers for that," I commented. "If all goes well, they could replenish the local population."

Muzo turned to speak at the tank. "Hear that, guys? Don't hold back on the sex!"

The snails wriggled their antennae.

Muzo nodded firmly. "I think they got the message."

I kept smiling at Muzo's earnest passion for the snails. How did I get so lucky?

"It's about time for their dinner. Would you like to feed them?" I asked.

He gasped. "I can feed them?"

To keep a seamless aesthetic in the room, I kept the tank supplies hidden in a ceiling compartment. Using the stepladder, I took out the food from a small mini fridge, then moved the stepladder next to the tank.

"Come up with me," I encouraged Muzo.

He scampered up to the top step, then paused. "Whoa. This is higher up than it looked from the floor."

"I've got you. I won't let you fall," I promised, putting my hand on his hip. "Would you like to do the honors?"

He grinned as he accepted the pail of food. I'd never seen anyone so excited to feed a snail—except for myself, of course.

"Wow, they've got a whole smorgasbord in here," Muzo said, glancing into the pail. "Cucumbers, bananas, apples, some leafy stuff... Do they get all of it?"

"They would explode if they ate all that. Let's do a slice of cucumber."

Muzo batted his eyelashes. "Maybe a slice of apple, too? For dessert?"

I couldn't resist those puppy-dog eyes. "Sure."

He took a slice of cucumber and apple from the pail and gently dropped them into the water. The offerings fell slowly until they landed on the rock outcropping right in front of the snails. They paused for a second before their antennae wriggled faster and they crept towards the food.

"They're going for it!" Muzo said, leaning forward.

I held him tighter so he wouldn't fall in. My fingers curled securely around his lithe waist, almost touching at the tips.

Our substantial size difference excited me. Since I was so big, I always figured I'd be larger than my omega mate, but not to this extent. Maybe it was my draconic predator urges twisting hunger into arousal. I could eat Muzo in one gulp if I wanted to—but obviously, I would never harm him. I held him closer, protecting him with my strong hands.

"What's up, Cobalt?" Muzo asked with a chuckle. "You trying to squeeze me like a tube of toothpaste?"

I loosened my grip. I hadn't realized I was holding him that tightly.

"Sorry," I murmured.

He craned his neck back to look up at me. Despite his vulnerable position, there was no fear in his gaze—not now, not ever. He only ever looked at me with love.

Muzo licked his lips, hesitating like he wanted to say something.

"What is it?" I asked.

"Could you take a step or two down?"

I complied with his suggestion. We were closer to eye-level now, although I was still a couple inches taller.

Then Muzo kissed me.

My brief surprise melted as our lips parted and our tongues brushed together. A velvety shiver shot through my veins, lighting a fire of arousal between my thighs. I kissed him deeper until his tiny moans of pleasure grew loud enough to echo off the tank glass.

When we parted for air, Muzo's eyelashes fluttered against his flushed cheeks. His dark eyes glittered with desire. Did he feel my hardening cock pressing against him earlier, or was our lust naturally synced up?

Either way, neither of us wanted to wait. I lifted Muzo off the stepladder and brought both of us to the floor.

"Hey," Muzo said, his voice husky. "You can partially shift, right?"

"Yes."

He glanced at my now fully hard cock straining in my pants. "Can you... pick and choose what body part you shift?"

I heard an idea rattling around in there.

"Tell me what you want," I said.

He swallowed visibly. "It was really hot when you brought your wings and claws out last time we had sex. So... I want to see your dragon cock on your human body."

My brows rose. I hadn't considered that option before. Was it even possible?

But I'd do anything for him, even if that meant stretching the limits of possibility.

"I can try," I said. "Step back."

Muzo stumbled to the corner of the room, his gaze eagerly locked on my lower half. I stripped out of my clothes. Despite my ravenous lust, I did it carefully this time since Crimson had gone through all that effort to dress me. When I was safely nude, I shut my eyes and focused on my inner dragon.

It didn't take much to lure him out. He was always ready to play.

I exhaled steadily as the shift came over me. I felt my body changing, growing. It was strange, but good.

I shuddered as the bottom half of my cock touched the cold floor. Was it that big already?

I couldn't tell when the shift finally stopped. It seemed to go on forever. It was Muzo's voice that alerted me to its finality.

"Your hair got long again," Muzo pointed out warmly.

I opened my eyes. A few wild strands fell in front of my vision. The same thing happened earlier. I must not have been able to fully control the partial dragon transformation.

Muzo stared at me, licking his lips. "You look so hot right now, Cobalt."

My lust flared. I wanted to dig my claws into my mate and fuck him silly, but it was literally impossible with my shifted cock. If my regular human erection wouldn't fit inside him, there was no way in hell this version would.

But when Muzo kneeled on the floor, I realized he had something else in mind.

The sight of my tiny mate beside my monstrous dragon cock was something I'd never forget. I twitched in anticipation, throbbing with need when he hadn't even touched me yet.

"Wow," Muzo said breathlessly. "I knew you'd be big, but this is crazy."

When he placed his soft palms on my cock, I hissed through my teeth. They felt sharp in my mouth—they must've shifted, too.

My body tensed as Muzo rubbed his hands along my length. The pleasure sparking in my veins was hot. Intense. The sensation was different to anything I'd felt before, and I couldn't get enough of it.

"Strip," I ordered in a throaty growl.

Muzo nodded, quickly tearing out of his clothes. When he kneeled back down, he was naked and hard.

"Get on top of it," I commanded.

Muzo's eyes flashed. He swung a leg over the girth of my cock and lowered himself until he was hugging it like a body pillow. His face was deeply flushed.

"L-like this?" he asked.

I grunted in affirmation. The lust warped my brain, making it difficult to speak. All I managed to get out was, "Pleasure yourself."

He nodded, then rocked his hips back and forth with a soft groan. The first couple hesitant motions quickly gave way to frantic, brainless thrusting. The lascivious way his cock rubbed against mine burned into my memory. I'd never forget the expression of wanton pleasure on my mate's face, or the electric sensation burning in my veins. Everything about it was so obscene, so perfectly filthy.

I tossed my head back. A thick growl vibrated in my throat as Muzo pleasured himself on me. The feedback loop was incredible. As he frotted against my dragon cock, I twitched and throbbed against his erection, making him gasp with need and rock his hips faster.

I wished for a surface for my claws to grab hold of— like bed sheets, destined to be ripped apart—but there was something intensely naughty about this position, standing upright with my dragon cock trailing on the floor while my mate grinded on me.

"Cobalt," Muzo said in a dazed whisper. His eyes fogged over with lust.

Fuck, my dragon wanted to bend him over and fill him to bursting.

"Finish on me," I demanded hoarsely.

He swallowed hard, nodding. Sweat dampened his hair, making loose strands of black and blond spill over his forehead. He was a beautiful, lust-addled mess.

His hips picked up speed. He moaned, his voice rising and falling with every movement. The room filled his scent —his natural body smell, his arousal, his breath, his sweat. I couldn't get enough of it.

"Cobalt," he whimpered, barely getting my name out. "I'm gonna..."

"Come for me. Do it."

A shudder wracked his body. He tensed, going stock-still, then let loose a scream of pleasure. He twitched and jerked, shooting out thick ropes of white across my sensitive flesh. He kept humping my cock as he came, chasing his pleasure to the very end. When it was over, he curled up, hugging my dragon dick like a pillow.

"Holy shit, that was amazing... What 'bout you?" he murmured, glancing up at me with remnants of lust in his eyes.

"Close. Stay there," I said through my fangs.

Muzo did as he was told, but he couldn't do it without being mischievous. He rubbed his arms up and down my sensitive shaft, using his whole body to get me off.

My mind was pure static. I couldn't take it. I felt like I was going to explode.

"Get a bucket," I ordered.

Muzo grinned devilishly. He ran to fetch an empty one, then kneeled by the head of my cock. Thank Holy Drake he understood what I meant without my explanation. I could barely think, let alone communicate.

Muzo delicately placed the tip of my cock past the rim

of the bucket. "There we go," he said, rubbing his hand along my sensitive head. "Let's see how much cum a dragon makes."

That was it.

His soft palm and filthy words pushed me over the brink. My roar blasted through the room, bouncing off the glass. The pleasure seizing my body was unbearable. A thick torrent of cum shot out of me. The force nearly knocked the bucket out Muzo's hand. He held it tight as he diligently stroked my twitching cock to completion.

Stars blurred my vision. My knees shook. I forced myself to breathe, otherwise I'd pass out.

Once the deluge of pleasure finally fizzled out, I felt my body returning to normal. My dragon was satisfied. My draconic features receded until I looked like a regular human again.

Muzo ran up and caught me before my legs gave out. "Whoa there, big guy," he said with a laugh. "You okay?"

I took a deep breath to clear my head. "Yes. I think so."

"Good, 'cause you're too big for me to hold upright forever."

I steadied myself, then smiled at my mate. "Thank you. I didn't realize I'd get so woozy after... that."

Muzo grinned like an imp. "Speaking of *that,* you seriously filled the whole bucket. I mean, wow. It was like a whole can of white paint."

My cheeks burned with embarrassment. Now that I wasn't horny, my actions seemed terribly lewd.

"I'm going to burn that thing," I mumbled.

Muzo cackled with laughter until he was doubled over. I'm glad *he* thought it was funny. Now I had one less usable bucket for my aquarium.

But for sex like that, I'd sacrifice it all over again.

TWENTY-ONE

Muzo

EXCITEMENT CHARGED the air as the contestants waited for the start of the third challenge. Apparently, competing for one million bucks was more inspiring than competing for an alpha dragon.

After Gaius led us into the forest, he announced they'd compete in a scavenger hunt for a particular prize. I looked around curiously at the gathered omegas. They seemed tense and eager in a different way than in previous challenges.

I felt bad that nobody else would get their shot at love this time. I remembered being in their shoes during the first two Dragonfate Games. But entering a game show wasn't a guarantee that an alpha was destined to fall in love with you. That was up to fate. I just got lucky this time— and I'd fallen in love with the alpha of my dreams.

"Well, you're looking particularly wistful today," Alaric remarked. He stood next to me in human form. I noticed his outfit was unusually rough around the edges. His white sleeves were rolled up, and his jeans looked like they'd been worn more than twice in their entire lifespan. Was he actually planning to participate this time?

"Yeah," I said.

He arched a brow. "I suppose you can afford to stand around and daydream, since you've won the Games already. You've got everything you could ever want."

I couldn't deny that. "Yup."

Alaric sighed. "There's no accounting for tact..."

"Sorry," I said, not wanting to make him feel bad. It didn't escape me that this was his third time on the Games and he hadn't found his mate yet. He'd always been competitive and ambitious. It must've sucked for him to 'lose' three times in a row.

"It's not your fault, but I appreciate the sentiment," Alaric said. "Cobalt isn't my type, anyway. Too much of a big, quiet lug."

"Yeah, he is," I said fondly.

"Why are you here, anyway?" Alaric asked, folding his arms. "This is a consolation challenge. Shouldn't you be at home with your man?"

A few nearby contestants turned to look at me. They must've been eavesdropping, wondering the same thing as Alaric.

"Oh, I'm not competing," I explained. "I'm just here to cheer you guys on. Jade said that was allowed. Something about narratives and good TV."

The contestants rolled their eyes and tuned out of the conversation. Guess I wasn't making any new friends on *this* season.

Alaric snorted, but there was a hint of humor in it. "I dare say the only person you're popular with is Cobalt."

"Hey, what about you and Poppy?" I asked, pouting.

"You're all right. For a dog," Alaric conceded with a smirk.

I grinned back. "Jackal."

"Yes, yes. Speaking of mildly irritating canines, where *is* Poppy?" Alaric asked.

I didn't see another head of white hair among the contestants. Usually he stayed close to me during the challenges. But since I'd already won Cobalt's heart, he didn't need to do that anymore.

"Emergency bathroom break?" I suggested.

Just as I piped up, a nearby group of rough voices spoke over me. They stood in a closed circle.

"Stay where you are. Yeah, right where we can see you," one contestant spat.

I couldn't see who they were talking to over the rest of the crowd. I exchanged a confused glance with Alaric. "What's that about?" I asked.

He narrowed his odd-colored eyes. "Sounds like trouble," he mumbled. He paused, sniffing the air. "Smell that?"

I followed his lead, then froze. Distinct fear scent muddied the air, mingled with another familiar scent that turned my blood to ice.

I rushed past the crowd and into the circle, using my small stature to squeeze past them.

"Hey!" somebody protested.

I sucked in a breath when I saw Poppy. He was hunched over, cowering in fear.

"Poppy!" I cried, rushing towards him. "What happened?"

He didn't look injured, but his brown eyes were glassy with fright. He relaxed slightly when I put my arms around him.

"N-nothing," Poppy murmured. "It's okay."

"You're shaking like a leaf, Pops."

He averted his gaze. "I always do that..."

I frowned, glancing at the circle of omegas

surrounding him. "Are these guys bothering you?" I asked my friend.

"No," Poppy lied.

I didn't get mad often, but bullies pissed me off—especially ones who picked on people as soft as Poppy. My pack animal instincts flared in my chest. My teeth shifted into fangs that I bared at the bullies.

"I don't know what you said to Poppy, but you'd better back off," I warned.

They glared at me, but hesitated. They all knew I was Cobalt's mate. Even if they didn't want me present, they couldn't do shit about it.

"Exactly what we thought would happen," one of the bullies muttered before the group dispersed.

Alaric sauntered up to us. "What happened?" he asked.

The uncomfortable atmosphere went back to normal, and the hairs on the back of my neck fell back down. "I dunno. What'd they say to you, Poppy?"

He stared at the ground. "They said... I'd better stay away from you during the challenge."

"What? Why?"

Poppy bit his lip. "They know we're friends. They said I'd use that as an unfair advantage to win. Like you'd give me tips on where the treasure is."

Alaric tilted his head at me. "*Do* you know?"

I scoffed. "No way! I didn't even know what the challenge was about 'til I got here."

"I said that, but nobody believed me," Poppy murmured.

I hugged him harder. "It's okay, Pops. Just ignore them."

"I agree," Alaric said. "Money makes people do stupid things. A large amount of money—like one million dollars—makes people do even stupider things."

Poppy smiled weakly. "Yeah. I'll try. Thanks, you two."

"What's going on here?"

My heart leapt at Cobalt's voice. I instantly felt safer and calmer knowing he was here.

"Everything's okay now, I think," I said. "Some guys were bugging Poppy."

Cobalt frowned. Without another word, he reached into his pocket and pulled out a small notepad and pen.

"Write down their names," Cobalt said quietly. "They won't be winning any prize money."

Alaric grinned. "Oh, my. He's scarier than I thought."

"Hey, back off, kitty cat. I already marked my territory," I teased.

But Poppy shook his head. "Please, it's okay. I-I don't want to hurt anyone's chances of winning money."

Cobalt slowly leaned down to Poppy's eye level and put a friendly hand on his shoulder. Poppy always seemed a bit nervous around alphas, but he didn't flinch away from Cobalt's gentle touch. Maybe it was because he was my mate, but Poppy seemed to understand Cobalt's intentions were good.

"It's my money, so I choose who does or doesn't receive it," Cobalt said. "And nobody who hurts or harasses you deserves the prize."

Poppy looked comforted by his words. "Okay..."

My heart swelled with affection for my mate. I loved that he was kind to my friends.

"Gaius looks ready to start," Cobalt remarked. "I'll be waiting. Coming, Muzo?"

"Yup." I hugged Poppy one last time. "Go get 'em, Pops. You too, Alaric."

Alaric shrugged at Poppy. "Sorry, wolf, but I intend to win. You're on your own for this one."

Poppy nodded in determination. "I-I'm gonna try to win, too."

I resumed my spot next to Cobalt as Gaius relayed the rules.

"All right, omegas!" Gaius began. "Your final task—for a prize of one million dollars—is to hunt down rare red moss. It could be anywhere on the island, but here's a hint from yours truly—think smarter, not harder." He winked. "You have two hours. If it's found, the winner will get the full cash prize. If nobody finds the moss by the time limit, the money will be divided among you."

Everyone murmured in excitement.

"Your time... starts *now!*" Gaius shouted.

"Rare red moss?" I asked, glancing up at Cobalt.

"It's for the snails," he explained. "My research tells me they use it for breeding."

"What, like a sex toy?"

The corner of his mouth curved in amusement. "No, as a substrate for eggs. But I see you've got some *creative* ideas." He lowered his voice, leaning a bit closer. "Though after what happened last night, I shouldn't be surprised."

Gaius poked his head into the conversation. "Ooh, what happened last night?"

A blush dusted Cobalt's cheeks. "None of your business," he mumbled.

"Excuse you," Gaius said with a scoff. "I'm the host, darling. Everything that happens during the show *is* my business."

Cobalt leveled a glare at him.

Gaius sighed, shaking his head. "No dice? Then I have no choice but to use my wild imagination..."

I chuckled, wondering what kind of wacky things Gaius would cook up in his mind, and how close they'd be to the truth.

Suddenly, I heard a small yelp. My lingering animal instincts stirred in my blood. I knew it was Poppy without even going to the source of the noise.

I immediately ran over to him. He sat at the mouth of a cavern in wolf form gingerly holding up one paw, as if he hurt himself.

"What happened?" I asked.

Poppy sighed, sounding exasperated with himself. "It's nothing. I just stepped on a sharp rock."

I wondered if he was still shaken up by the bullies and hadn't been paying attention to his surroundings. If the challenge just started and he already hurt his paw, would he be safe wandering around alone? What if the bullies came back?

"I'm coming with you, Pops," I announced.

His eyes widened. "W-what? You can't. People will think you're helping me."

"Let 'em think whatever they want. I don't have any secret knowledge, so how could I help? I'm only gonna keep you company, that's all."

Poppy's fur flattened in relief. "Oh, Muzo... Thank you."

Cobalt ran over with a concerned frown. Behind him trailed a camera-wielding kobold.

"What's going on?" Cobalt asked.

"I'm going with Poppy on the scavenger hunt." I looked directly at the camera. "Not helping. Just accompanying." I took off my shirt and handed it to Cobalt. "Here, hold my clothes."

After stripping, I shifted to jackal form and pressed my fur against Poppy's side. I felt his heartbeat slow down.

"All right," Cobalt said, eyeing me in concern. "Be careful. Both of you."

I snorted. "It's just a scavenger hunt. We'll be fine. See ya in two hours!"

Cobalt nodded at the cameraman to follow us. I figured it was less for TV and more for our safety. My alpha was such a worrywart sometimes.

"Lead the way, Pops," I said.

He glanced around nervously. "All right. Um... When I think of moss, I think of caves. How about in here?" he asked, pointing his nose towards the cavern.

Cobalt mentioned the Chromatimaeus river snails used the moss for breeding, so it must be somewhere wet. Didn't most caves contain some water? Poppy's idea was a good one, but since I wasn't supposed to help, I didn't share my thoughts.

I shrugged. "Hey, don't ask me. I'm just along for the ride. Wherever you go, I go."

"Okay."

The two of us padded into the yawning mouth of the cavern. It was dark and damp inside. The rich smell of earth surrounded us, along with the scent and sound of water coming from deeper within. That lifted my hopes. Could Poppy find the rare moss after all?

Poppy raised his head to sniff the air, then set off towards the water. Along the way, he asked, "So, how's it going with Cobalt?"

I grinned. "Awesome. He's the best."

"Is he nice? He seems nice," Poppy said wistfully.

"'Course he's nice! I wouldn't be fated to some douchebag."

"That's good." He sighed in relief. "Oh Muzo, I'm so happy for you. I was really worried what would happen if you had to leave the island and go back to nothing..."

I headbutted his shoulder. "Hey, I wouldn't have *nothing*. I'd have you."

He smiled, gently thumping his tail against me. "I know. But with my earnings, I couldn't feed you and put a roof over your head forever. That's why I'm glad Cobalt is your mate. He'll always take care of you."

Warmth filled my chest. Cobalt had said the same thing to me. I'd never felt as safe and secure as I did with him—not just in terms of money, but *everything*. He was my home.

But I felt a twinge of guilt, too. Taylor found his mate in Crimson, and now I'd found my mate in Cobalt. It wasn't fair that our sweet Poppy was still alone.

I licked my friend's cheek. "You'll find your mate, Pops, I promise. And he's gonna be the nicest, gracious-est, most pleasant and respectable guy you ever did meet!"

"W-what are you talking about?" Poppy huffed. "Enough about me. I want to know more about you two." He dropped into a whisper. "Did you... you know..."

"Did we what? Oh. Have sex? Yeah, a bunch of times."

If Poppy was in human form, a blush would've lit up his whole face. Instead his fur fluffed out around his neck. "Y-you did? Wait, Muzo. Are you pregnant?"

I blanked. *Was* I pregnant? I didn't know. We talked about breeding and never used protection, so it wasn't impossible.

"Uh," I said. "Maybe?"

Poppy's tail wagged vigorously. "Muzo! I can't believe you're going to be a parent. Oh, that's so wonderful."

It hadn't struck me until now that—yeah, I *was* going to be a parent.

And Poppy was right. It *was* wonderful.

I couldn't help wagging my tail, too. "Yeah. It's early, but I'm pretty excited about it. I can't wait for my kid to meet Uncle Tay and Uncle Pops."

Poppy beamed, looking absolutely elated. He opened his mouth to say something, but was cut off by a sneering voice.

"I fucking knew it. Look, the jackal's leading him right to the prize!"

We spun around to see a trio of contestants behind us. There were two wolves, one brown and one gray, and a coyote. Since I was a jackal and Poppy was a relatively small wolf, all three of them outmatched us in size.

I felt a zap of recognition. Their forms were different, but there was no mistaking their voices and foreboding attitudes. These were the same bullies harassing Poppy earlier.

My hackles rose into furry spikes. "What do you want?" I demanded.

"We want the prize," the brown wolf growled. "Tell us where the moss is."

I scoffed. "Geez, you guys are stubborn. I don't know jack shit."

The gray wolf bared his fangs. "Don't play dumb. Or maybe you just *are* dumb."

The insult made me snort with laughter. I'd heard way worse from Alaric. These bullies would have to try harder to upset me.

"Yeah, yeah," I said. "Let's not start a dog fight over some moss, okay?"

"It's not about the damned moss," the coyote snarled. "It's about a million dollars. Split three ways, we'll be set."

The two wolves exchanged a subtle glance. Geez, did they plan on shutting out the coyote shifter? These guys really sucked.

I shrugged. "I dunno what to tell you. Seriously, you're better off looking elsewhere instead of following us."

"I'm sorry. Muzo really doesn't know where it is," Poppy murmured. "So, please, leave us alone."

"Hey, don't apologize to these dudes," I said.

Poppy's voice came out as a soft whimper. "I'm sorry..."

"Enough whining already," the brown wolf barked. His voice echoed off the narrow cave walls. "If you really want us to leave, then tell us where the moss is. Now."

I wasn't worried about an actual fight. The bullies wouldn't dare harm either of us on tape. The camera guy was still present, hiding along the shadowy cave wall while filming. At least, I think he was. It was difficult to tell with all the bodies in the way.

But that didn't stop Poppy from trembling. He shivered violently, flattening his belly to the ground in terror.

And *that* pissed me off.

"Screw you, dickhead," I snapped, stepping in front of Poppy. "Leave him alone."

The brown wolf lunged closer, his spittle flying across my face. "What the hell did you just call me?" he shouted. His roar echoed louder this time, ricocheting violently off the walls.

Suddenly, the floor rumbled beneath my paw pads. The entire cavern groaned. Dirt showered from the ceiling.

My heart leapt into my throat.

The narrow cavern chamber was about to collapse.

"Shit. Run!" the brown wolf yelled.

As he bolted away, a torrent of dirt landed where he'd been a second earlier.

I skittered backwards. Poppy yelped with fright.

Within seconds, the light at the end of the tunnel disappeared, and everything went dark.

TWENTY-TWO

Cobalt

—————————

"PREGNANT?" Gaius said, his eyes going wide. "Did Muzo just say he's pregnant?"

I stared at the live feed in disbelief. I'd been glued to the screen since Poppy and Muzo disappeared into the cavern twenty minutes ago, but the sudden topic of our relationship—and Muzo's possible pregnancy—caught me by surprise.

"He could be," I admitted, my heart fluttering at the idea.

Gaius let out a hearty laugh and slapped me on the shoulder. "Cobalt, you dog! You couldn't even wait until the Games ended!" He put a finger to his chin thoughtfully. "Actually, all three of you did the deed during the show, didn't you? You naughty dragons just can't keep it in your pants."

I waved a hand at Gaius to shush him. He was speaking over Poppy and Muzo's conversation, and I wanted to hear everything.

But when a trio of omegas appeared on screen, Gaius quieted down on his own. He watched with a frown that was mirrored on my own face. It quickly became clear what was going on. They were there to harass my mate.

Anger twisted like thorns in my chest. How dare they?

I stood in a hurry, ready to run into the cavern after Muzo and teach those assholes a lesson they'd never forget.

Gaius grabbed my arm. "Cobalt," he said, his tone uncharacteristically grave. "Look."

The horrible scene unfolded in slow motion. The tense argument, the shaking camera, the onslaught of collapsing earth, then finally, an all-encompassing cloud of dust.

The live feed cut off from Muzo and Poppy.

They were alone in the caved-in tunnel.

My *pregnant mate* was in danger.

Hot fury exploded within me. In a heartbeat, my dragon tore free from my human flesh. The surrounding trees crumpled when my wings snapped open and my tail cracked like a whip. The earth yielded beneath me as my full weight manifested under my claws.

Unfortunately, Gaius was caught in the crossfire of my chaotic shift. He lay flat on his back under a mess of broken branches. He coughed, pushing a twig out of his face. There was a small cut on his cheek, but otherwise he appeared to be in one piece, thank Holy Drake. It terrified me that I could have killed him by accident.

"Gaius, are you—"

"I'm fine, you great big oaf," he assured me, getting to his feet and dusting himself off. "Go save Muzo and Poppy."

I nodded swiftly, then leapt towards the cavern. My careful instincts had served me well. I stayed nearby out of concern for my mate, so it only took a couple pumps of my wings to reach the site.

Panic fueled me. I raked my claws across the top of the buckled cavern, tossing the loose earth out of the way. Fear ran cold in my veins when nothing came of it. No matter how much dirt I shovelled aside, all that emerged was more packed earth.

My mate.

Where *was* he?

A dreadful scream-like roar ripped loose from my throat. I couldn't lose him. I had to save him, no matter what. My body ran on instinct and desperation as I combed through the remains of the tunnel.

I sucked in a hopeful breath when a brownish canine head popped out of the dirt. But it wasn't a jackal. It wasn't my Muzo. It was a coyote, one of the bullies. It took every ounce of willpower to restrain myself from crushing him like an insect.

But my rage subsided slightly when the coyote spat out a mouthful of dirt and said, "Over there! Those two were further that way!"

He pointed to a section of the cave that went deeper underground. I left him and followed the length of the tunnel, frantically clawing through the walls.

I cursed myself. Not again. This couldn't happen again. I couldn't fail and let my loved ones get hurt. What good was my massive size and my raw power if I couldn't even help my mate with them?

The uppermost part of the cavern was gone. The only thing remaining was the underground tunnel, and every time I pawed through a section of it, nothing and nobody turned up. My stomach flipped. How deep could they possibly have gone? Or were they buried under a heap of rubble?

It wasn't working. I had to try something else. I thrust my long neck into the tunnel, blinking rapidly to adjust to the darkness.

But then I saw *something*.

Red. A huge pool of red.

My heart tripped over itself in shock and terror. Was that blood?

But as light poured in from above, I saw something else. Within the red circle was a fluffy yellow-white figure curled up tightly in a ball.

"Poppy," I cried, my dragon voice booming in the underground chasm.

His ears flicked up. Slowly, he raised his head and blinked his wide brown eyes, then gasped. "Cobalt!"

Although I was relieved to see him safe, that didn't ease my panic. My mate was nowhere to be seen.

"Where's Muzo?" I asked.

I heard a familiar grunt of effort before a pair of pointy ears popped up from between Poppy's paws. Poppy unfurled his body to reveal a very dirty but living Muzo.

He shook out his pelt. "Okay, if there's one thing I hate getting in my nose more than sand, it's dirt. Blech."

"Muzo," I said, my voice breaking with heart-wrenching relief.

My mate grinned like he'd just had an amazing adventure instead of a near-death experience. "Hey, Cobalt!"

I reached my paw carefully through the tunnel to pick them up. Poppy happily climbed aboard, but Muzo stayed inside the red circle.

"Wait, wait. Check this out," he said, pawing at it. "Red moss! Isn't this what we were looking for?"

I did a double take. I'd been so worried about my mate I hadn't even recognized the moss, but Muzo was correct. The substance beneath them was the rare red moss needed for the river snails.

I was still so shaken with relief I could barely speak. "How did you...?"

Muzo was all too eager to explain. "So, when the cave-in happened, Poppy grabbed me by the scruff and used his body like a shield."

Poppy looked embarrassed. "You just told me you were pregnant. I had to protect you."

I felt an immense rush of gratitude towards Poppy. I was lucky my mate had such incredible friends.

"But the blast from the cave-in sent us flying down this tunnel," Muzo went on. "That's when we landed on this bed of moss. Pretty nifty, huh? It's like destiny or something."

I let out a relieved laugh.

It was destiny, all right.

"WHAT DO you mean you want to split the prize?" Muzo blurted.

He and Poppy were dressed in fresh clothes after being rescued from the caved-in tunnel. My dragon transformation had ripped my clothes into shreds, so I got a new outfit, too. Good thing I hadn't worn Crimson's custom-made suit today. His heart couldn't handle any more clothing-related disasters.

The challenge was over. Everyone had gathered at the starting point to hear Gaius and I announce the winner of the coveted prize. I did my best not to glare at the trio of troublemakers who'd harassed my mate and his friend in the cavern. They hung their heads, their faces drawn with guilt. They looked like they were about to get the verbal smack-down of their lives.

Although they'd technically both landed on the moss at the same time, Muzo wasn't participating, so Poppy was the true winner. That entitled him to the million-dollar prize.

Except...

"I don't want it," Poppy said firmly. "Not the whole thing."

Muzo gaped at him like he had two heads. "Pops, it's a million bucks! You'd be set for life."

"I'm splitting it," Poppy insisted. "It's too much money for me. I'd feel better if it was distributed evenly."

The other contestants stared at him in astonished awe. Not counting Muzo, there were fourteen remaining omegas—including the bullies. A million dollars split evenly among each contestant was still a handsome sum of money, and a nice consolation prize for competing in the Games.

"If that's what you want, Poppy, we'll make it happen," I promised. Then I tapped the notebook in my pocket and murmured, "Just remember what I said earlier."

But Poppy met my gaze evenly. "I want it split among *everyone*."

I sighed. My inner dragon didn't understand how this soft-hearted wolf could be so compassionate even to people who wronged him. But it was Poppy's decision, and I'd honor it, even if I didn't agree with it.

"All right," I said.

Muzo heaved a sigh. "Man, you are way too nice for your own good, Pops."

Alaric strode towards us with his arms folded across his chest. "I'm inclined to agree," he muttered, shooting a nasty glare at the trio in question. "You're far more forgiving than I would've been."

"Somebody has to be," Poppy said, his soft words almost defiant.

Gaius flounced into the scene. He sported a new dirt-free Hawaiian shirt, and the scratch on his cheek was covered up by skilfully applied foundation. "Wow, what a wild ride—and an exciting end to the challenge! The jackal found his fated mate, the alpha dragon found his mate *and* his moss, and the benevolent white wolf shared his winnings with everyone. You never know what's going to happen on the Dragonfate Games, folks!"

TWENTY-THREE

Muzo

AFTER THE CLOSING ceremony wrapped up and filming concluded, season three of the Dragonfate Games was officially over. And for the first time ever, I didn't have to go back home at the end—because I was already home.

It felt weird standing on the beach and saying goodbye to Poppy. We'd always lost the Games together. We left the island together. We sat next to each other on the plane. We hung out all the time back in the human city. But now I belonged here, on Chromatimaeus Island. That chapter of our lives was over.

Taylor—my other best friend turned brother-in-law, via dragon mate shenanigans—joined me for moral support. He was always the rock in our trio's friendship. His presence was the only thing stopping me from bursting into tears.

Well, it did for about five minutes, and then I started bawling anyway. Maybe it was the pregnancy hormones—confirmed, thanks to a pee-on-a-stick test—but I was a freaking wreck. I clung to Poppy and soaked his shirt with tears. He was pretty sensitive too, so my crying made *him* cry.

Taylor patted both of us on the back as we hugged. "There, there, you guys. It's okay. It's not like you're never going to see each other again."

I gasped, sniffing loudly. "But what if we don't?"

"You know Poppy is always welcome here, Dragonfate Games or not," Cobalt reassured me. He was there to support me, along with Crimson, Taylor's mate. The alpha dragons both knew we three omegas had a special friendship.

"R-really?" Poppy asked, his doe eyes watery.

Crimson scoffed in amusement. "Really, he asks, as if he hasn't been invited to every season of the Games. By the way, the offer still stands for next time."

Cobalt nodded. "Say the word and I'll book your flight, no TV show required," he promised with a smile. "I owe you for saving Muzo's life. I'll be forever in your debt."

Poppy flashed a grateful smile in return.

"Can't you just stay here on the island?" I asked, pouting. "There's tons of spare rooms in the castle."

Poppy shook his head. "It's all right, Muzo. I have a life to get back to, and with the prize money, things will be easier." He hugged his friend tighter. "Don't worry about me. I'll see you soon—and the baby, too."

A warm feeling bloomed in my chest. The next time I saw Poppy, I'd have laid my egg and seen it hatch already. My baby would exist in the world, bright-eyed and beautiful.

"Okay," I said, calmer now as I brushed the tears away. "But you'd better hurry up and fall in love with a dragon, okay?"

Poppy laughed softly. "I'll try my best."

A FEW WEEKS had passed since the Games ended, and living in the lap of luxury was finally starting to feel real.

It was the perfect beach day. Sunlight made the white sand glitter like diamonds, and the ocean was a picturesque shade of blue. The whole family gathered on the beach for a barbecue to celebrate my pregnancy, which was a pretty damn sweet thing to do.

I lounged in my pillow-padded chair, wriggling my toes in the warmth of the sun. It was nice to finally enjoy the beach without having to do any challenges.

But the most awesome part about the family BBQ was that *Cobalt* did the barbecuing. He wore the adorable "Kiss the Cook" apron Taylor sewed for him back when he first moved in with the dragons.

As Cobalt set up the grill, it reminded me of my burger flipping days. I'd never forget that charred burger patty from my final shift...

"Do you want help?" I'd asked Cobalt, reaching for the spatula.

"No," he'd rumbled, holding the spatula high in the air, out of my reach. "You go sit down and relax. Let me do the cooking."

So I'd plopped my butt down in my comfy chair. But even while relaxing, I couldn't take my eyes off my mate. He looked sexy as hell manning the grill.

Saffron sat in the beach chair next to me. He leaned closer. "So, Muzo. Now that you're part of the fam, are you gonna spill Cobalt's secret?"

"What secret?" I asked, munching on a pre-BBQ strip of jerky. The pregnancy had amped up my appetite to eleven.

Saffron waved a hand. "You know. His hoard. You've seen it, right?"

I blinked as memories of the cum bucket flashed before my eyes. "Uh."

Thystle snorted as he pulled up the adjacent two chairs for himself and his mate, Matteo.

"Don't bother telling him, Muzo," Thystle said. "He's only going to make fun of it like he does with everyone else's hoard."

"Hey, I don't make fun of yours anymore, emo boy," Saffron argued. "Not since I saw Matteo live on stage. He was awesome."

Matteo grinned as he sat next to Thystle. "Thanks."

"You *were* awesome," Thystle agreed, kissing Matteo on the cheek before turning back to his brother. "Anyway, if Cobalt wants to keep his hoard a secret, let him. Don't feel peer-pressured to spill anything, Muzo."

Saffron groaned. "Aw, come on! Look, I'll trade you, info for info. I hoard movies, Aurum's is video games, Jade obviously hoards books, and Viol's is—"

Viol's ominous voice cut in. "If you want to keep your tongue, stop using it."

Saffron yelped, nearly leaping out of his skin. He went pale as Viol loomed darkly behind him. "Fuck, where do you *come* from sometimes?" Saffron blurted.

Viol ignored him, looking to Matteo. "Where's Heather?" he asked gruffly.

Matteo gave a casual nod towards the sand, as if Viol hadn't just threatened to cut someone's tongue off. "Playing with Ruby. Taylor and Crimson are babysitting."

A frown etched into Viol's mouth. He looked disappointed, like a kid who couldn't have a cookie. He suddenly turned to me. "When are you due?" he asked.

Math was never my strong suit, and time slipped away on this dreamy island paradise. "Uh... A few weeks? Not sure," I admitted.

"How can you not be sure? You're growing an egg inside you," Viol retorted, sounding more confused than anything else.

I grinned, patting my belly. "Sure am. Man, it makes me hungry, though. Were you always starving, Matteo?"

Matteo tilted his head. "Not starving, but I craved my favorite food all the time." With a playful smirk at Thystle, he added, "And my mate was happy to feed it to me."

Viol's lip twitched. For a second, I almost thought he looked jealous.

I perked up as Cobalt approached me with a big, steaming plate of food. I swallowed to stop myself from drooling.

"Heard you're hungry," Cobalt said with a knowing smile. "I made a lot, so eat up."

I happily accepted the plate. The scents of sizzling meats and veggies wafted up to my nose, making my stomach growl louder. To my joy, half the plate was big, juicy grilled shrimp. Cobalt knew exactly what I loved. I didn't hesitate to shovel them in my mouth.

"Hey, what about the rest of us?" Saffron asked, glancing hungrily at my shrimp.

Cobalt shot him a look. "Pregnant omegas eat first."

"It's okay, he can have a bite," I said, offering a shrimp to Saffron. He looked as happy as a dog being fed scraps under the table.

I was about to offer a shrimp to Viol too, but he'd disappeared without another word. He must've slipped back into the shadows he manifested from.

"You guys want some?" I asked Thystle and Matteo.

Matteo reclined in his seat. "I'm good, thanks. I'm saving myself for sashimi."

Saffron snorted. "It's a barbecue, bro. That's like the opposite of what you want."

Tilting his head at his mate, Matteo put on a sly grin. "I guess Thystle will have to fetch it for me, then."

Thystle was already halfway out of his seat, ready to cater to his mate's every whim. "You *know* I can't resist that sexy voice…"

"And I can't resist that sexy face," Matteo teased back. "I'll come with you."

After the couple left, Cobalt sat by the foot of my chair. "Well? How is it?" he asked, examining my face hopefully.

"Mmm. *So* good," I said, snatching another shrimp. "You should cook more often, Cobalt. That apron looks sexy on you."

His cheeks flushed. "Oh." He cleared his throat. "I had no idea."

I looked him up and down, soaking in the sight of my mate. "Maybe you can wear it tonight?" I suggested.

"Guys, I'm right here," Saffron reminded us dryly. "Love that you're in love, but I don't need a live viewing of your sex tape."

Cobalt turned to him. "Then feel free to leave."

Saffron gawked. "Holy Drake, who's this pervert and what's he done with my big brother?"

Cobalt smirked at me. There was an undercurrent of desire gleaming in his deep blue gaze.

"Maybe he's been here all along," Cobalt remarked, staring directly into my eyes with such intensity that it sent a shiver down my spine.

Saffron's seat clattered as he rose from it. "Yup. And that's my cue to escape."

TWENTY-FOUR

Cobalt

———————

THERE WERE two cues that Muzo neared his egg-laying date.

One was his obviously enlarged appearance. His tiny body was stretched to the limit accommodating a massive dragon egg.

But the second was the change in his behavior. His easily distracted personality disappeared. He was solely focused on one thing—nesting.

"Why isn't there any dirt in this castle?" he grumbled, pacing around the bedroom. He'd woken up five minutes ago, but instead of his usual thoughts of breakfast, he kept insisting he needed dirt. It wasn't until I recalled Taylor and Matteo's strange pre-egg-laying habits that I realized it was nearly Muzo's time. If Taylor hoarded blankets and Matteo created a rooftop nest, then Muzo's obsession for dirt wasn't too farfetched.

"There are house cleaners whose job is to keep dirt *out* of the castle," I reminded him. "But if you want, I can make it happen."

He blinked at me, wide-eyed. "You can?"

I put my hand on his shoulder to ease his restless energy. "I'd make *anything* happen for you. You know that."

He nodded. "Okay, yeah, true. I mean, I don't want to get the bedroom dirty, but..." He bit his lip, trailing off. He clearly felt an urge he couldn't put into words. It must've been his jackal instincts.

"Muzo, we've done plenty of dirty things in this room, remember?" I teased.

He snorted, slapping my arm playfully. "Not like *that.*" He gasped as if an idea struck him. "Wait, wait. Isn't there, like, a garden or something?"

"Sure," I said, not quite understanding.

Then he ran out of the room at a speed I thought would be impossible given the size of his belly.

Spurred on by his urgency, I followed him outside the castle. I didn't want to leave him alone, not when he was so close to laying. This was when he needed the most protection. It didn't matter that the island full of dragons was the safest place on the planet for my mate—my instincts dictated that I had to be by his side.

Just as Muzo turned a corner ahead, a door opened in front of me and I crashed into the figure emerging from it. Judging by the yellow hair, it was one of the twins, but I was in too much of a hurry to focus on the hue, so I didn't know which one.

"Ow," the crashed-into twin complained, rubbing his head. "Dude, Cobalt, what's the rush? Is the house on fire?"

"Muzo's nesting," I explained quickly before bolting down the hall.

My chest swirled with anxiety and excitement. I needed to protect my mate, and I was also eager to see our beautiful egg. But first, I had to help Muzo through the process of laying it.

I found him behind the castle in the curated garden space. He wasn't hard to spot—the furry tail sticking out of a freshly dug hole in the ground was a good indication.

I sighed, relieved to catch up with him. "Need help?" I offered.

He didn't respond. He was muttering to himself about the size of the den, and how it had to be just right.

Instead of smothering him with assistance he didn't want, I waited beside the dirt pile like a bodyguard. I was content to watch him exert his natural urges. His jackal-isms were adorable.

"Ah," Jade said, appearing from behind a dragon-shaped topiary. He closed the book in his hand. There was a photo of various wild canines on the cover. "Looks like Muzo is right on time to start denning."

I blinked, surprised to see him. Before I could ask how he knew, Jade supplied the answer. "Aurum told us. The others are on their way with supplies if needed."

So the twin I'd run into was Aurum? I didn't expect him to raise the alarm, given his distaste for fated mates, but I supposed an egg-laying and the arrival of a new family member was different.

Right on cue, my brothers appeared, with mates in tow for those who had them. In their arms were blankets, towels, buckets of water, and everything else a nesting omega could ever need.

I kneeled closer to the opening of the rapidly forming den. "Muzo, everyone's here to help," I told him.

His distracted voice returned as a muffled echo from inside the dirt hole. "Wha? Oh, that's great, thanks."

Taylor clicked his tongue. His arms were full of scorned quilts. "We rushed for nothing. He's doing a fine job on his own."

Matteo shrugged casually. "Better to be over-prepared, eh?"

I nodded. Even if Muzo was fine, I appreciated both of them coming. I felt better knowing there were two omegas present who could walk my mate through the process if he needed moral support.

After twenty minutes of silent digging, Muzo's dusty jackal snout suddenly popped out of the hole. He looked frantic.

"What's wrong?" I asked.

"Blueberry," Muzo mumbled. "Where is he? Need Blueberry. Now."

"He wants blueberries?" Matteo asked, glancing at the nearest bush. "There's a whole patch of them there."

"No," I said, standing up. "He wants Blueberry, his plush toy. I'll go get him."

I last recalled seeing the plushie in our bedroom, where he sat by the headboard like the draconic king of Pillow Mountain.

There was no time to waste. If my mate wanted Blueberry, then I'd fetch him ASAP. I ran inside, up the stairs, and into our bedroom.

Only to find Blueberry missing.

Dumbfounded, I stared at the empty space. Blueberry was *always* there. But where could an inanimate object possibly have gone? It wasn't like he got up and walked away.

I tore the room apart looking for him, but to my frustration, I came up empty-handed. Muzo was waiting for me *and* Blueberry, but it pained me to be apart from my mate for a second longer.

"Sorry, Blueberry," I mumbled under my breath.

I raced back to the den in the garden. As my brothers made space for my return, I noticed one was missing—

Viol. In normal circumstances, I wouldn't have thought anything of it. But oddly, he never missed an egg-laying. It was the closest thing we had to quality family time with him.

But Viol wasn't my concern. My focus was on my mate.

Muzo heard my arrival and poked his head out of the den. "Did you find him?" he asked, eyes wide in anticipation.

I hated telling him my answer. "I'm sorry."

Muzo's face fell. He groaned and slunk back into the den, his sniffling cries echoing in the underground chamber. "No, no, no! I can't do this without him!"

At that moment, I wished I was smaller. I could've curled up with Muzo in his den. But I was too large, as both a human and a dragon.

That didn't mean I couldn't try.

I lowered myself to my knees, then placed my belly on the ground so my face was inside the den's opening.

"Muzo," I called. "I'm here."

In the darkness, I saw his watery eyes sparkle. He sniffled again. "Cobalt..."

He touched our noses together. His was wet and cold.

"Hi," I said.

That made him laugh. "Hi."

"I'm sorry about Blueberry, but I hope I can help instead."

"It's okay. I'm glad you're here."

It was difficult to see in the dark, but I heard him shuffle closer, then felt his whiskers brush against my face. His fur was warm. I wished I could shrink and cuddle him inside the den, but this was nice, too.

Suddenly, I felt a nudge in my side. Viol's voice came a second later.

"Hey. Get back out here for a sec," he ordered.

Confused, I wriggled back out of the den. Viol immediately thrusted Blueberry into my hands.

"Where did you find him?" I asked.

Viol scoffed. "Does it matter? Just give him to Muzo
already."

I wasn't about to look a gift plushie in the mouth. I
handed Blueberry to Muzo, whose eyes lit up.

"Ah! You found him!" Muzo cried.

He snatched the plushie in his teeth, then disappeared
down the dark hole.

My instincts told me Muzo had everything under
control. I stood back up and brushed the dirt off my shirt.
We all stood around the den quietly, waiting for any sign of
the egg.

Aurum cleared his throat loudly to break the silence.
"So, uh... Where *did* you find that plushie, Viol?" he
asked.

Viol glared at him. "None of your fucking business."

Saffron smirked. He stood elbow to elbow with his twin
to back him up. "Yeah, but it's Cobalt's business. And
mine, since I'm commissioning Taylor to make me a
plushie, too. I deserve to know about plushie-related crime
in my area."

Viol scowled at both of them. "There was no fucking
crime, okay?"

"Avoiding the accusations, I see," Aurum said slyly.

"What accusations?" Viol snarled.

The twins cackled and danced out of range as Viol
lunged at them.

Taylor raised an amused brow. In a quiet voice, he said,
"You know, Viol, if you want a mini dragon of your own,
you could always just ask me."

Viol's face paled and flushed at the same time. He was

beyond flustered. It was like Taylor had slapped him instead of offering to sew him a toy.

"I didn't—I don't—" Viol huffed loudly. "Fuckin' hell, I'm out. Someone tell me when the egg's here," he mumbled before stalking off like a cranky teenager.

When he was gone, Thystle rubbed his temple. "I am so confused. Did our vicious edgelord brother steal a plush toy from a pregnant omega?"

"I haven't the slightest," Crimson drawled. "And honestly? I don't want to know."

Jade smiled. "Whatever happened, the plushie returned to its rightful owner in the end, and that's what matters."

Ignoring the plushie debate, I stared at the den's entrance. Muzo had been quiet for a while. What was going on down there?

I kneeled down to the hole, but I couldn't see anything.

"Muzo? Are you okay?" I asked.

He didn't respond for a few beats. My chest clenched.

Then his cracked voice piped up, a whisper in the darkness: "It's... coming."

My heart skipped. The egg was coming. Would he get it out safely?

There was nothing I could do but trust my fated mate and wait.

I didn't dare blink as I watched the den opening for any sign of progress. Each second passed torturously slowly, while every beat of my heart quickened.

A low, pained groan came from within the den. My body went rigid.

"Muzo?" I called.

A few seconds later, a soft blue glow lit the den's darkness.

The egg.

I gasped, throwing myself on the ground and scrambling to see inside the den. I was greeted by Muzo's jackal grin. He looked exhausted, but happy.

And he wasn't alone. With the egg's glow lighting up the space, I could actually see inside. Curled up next to Muzo was Blueberry, of course—and the beautiful blue egg.

Our baby.

I was speechless. It was magnificent. The smooth shell gleamed like it was carved from pure sapphire.

"I did it," Muzo said breathlessly.

"You did, Muzo. I'm so proud of you," I murmured, my voice thick with emotion.

"And look how big it is!"

I chuckled as I reached out to stroke his cheek. "It *is* big. You did an amazing job."

He beamed with pride and joy, nuzzling his head into my palm.

"So, are you going to stay in here with the egg until it hatches?" I asked. Secretly, I worried I wouldn't see much of him until the baby emerged. As much as I wanted to encourage his natural instincts, I couldn't bear to be apart from my mate for that long. I'd need to set up camp outside in the garden...

Fortunately, Muzo shook his head. "Nope. Now that the egg's here, I don't have that nagging denning urge anymore." He grinned sheepishly. "Sorry for digging a huge hole in your garden."

I pressed a kiss to his cold nose. "Never apologize for following your instincts. Now, let's get you and our egg out of there."

"And Blueberry," Muzo reminded me, pawing at the dirt-covered plushie.

"And Blueberry," I agreed.

TWENTY-FIVE

Muzo
———

I YAWNED as Cobalt paced around the bedroom, wringing his hands. He'd been nervous all morning, despite my best efforts at reassurance, but it was one of those situations that wouldn't stop bugging him until he got it over with.

"Hey, Cobalt. Why don't you come hug the egg?" I suggested. "Might calm you down."

He stopped pacing and looked my way, his expression softening. "Yes. That's a good idea."

He walked over to the bed—which had all but disappeared under the pile of Taylor's lovingly sewn quilts—and sat beside me. I was all comfy in my pyjamas, curled up with the egg in my lap.

"How is it?" he asked, stroking the egg's round shell.

I yawned again. "Same as usual. Egging around."

"No movement?"

"Not yet."

Cobalt examined the surface. "And no pips." He sighed. "It should've pipped by now..."

I grabbed my mate's face. "C'mon, it's okay. Chill out. This stuff takes time, right?"

"Right," he murmured, although he was still pouting. The childish expression on his usually mature, stoic face was adorable.

"Besides, it's not really the egg you're worried about," I pointed out. "You're anxious about showing your brothers your hoard."

He pouted harder. "Yes."

I smiled. "It's gonna be okay, 'cause everything *always* works out in the end."

Cobalt met my gaze, then sighed and broke into a small smile. "If there's anything I've learned being your mate, Muzo, it's that your overly optimistic mantra is true."

"Aww, I'm rubbing off on you—and not in a sexual way."

Cobalt let out a snort of amusement seconds before a knock came at the door. He leapt out of bed.

"They're here."

"You can do it," I reassured him. "I'd come with you, but I gotta watch the egg."

The ginormous egg definitely inherited Cobalt's genes. It was too big for me to carry for long periods of time, so I'd have to sit the hoard tour out. But that was all right. Since Cobalt's hoard was literally in the next room, I still felt involved in the whole process.

Cobalt blew out a long breath and nodded. "Okay."

He opened the door.

The twins were closest. Birthday hats were strapped to their heads and party horns stuck out of their mouths. They blew on them simultaneously, making a pair of comical sounds. The streamers from the party horns slapped Cobalt's chest.

"Happy hoard reveal day!" the twins cried simulta-neously.

Cobalt shot me a miserable glance over his shoulder. "I knew this was a bad idea..."

"Where is it?" Aurum demanded, pushing past Cobalt into the room.

Saffron bounded inside. "Yeah, we wanna see!"

Crimson, Thystle, and Jade followed, although with less over-the-top enthusiasm. I didn't see Viol. Maybe he already knew about Cobalt's hoard—or he just didn't care.

"Yo, Muzo, give us a hint," Aurum said, poking my shoulder.

Saffron sat next to me. "Yeah, give us a hint. By the way, how's the egg? Hatching yet?"

I did a zipping motion across my mouth. "My lips are sealed. Just like the eggshell."

They both frowned in various shades of disappointment.

Crimson gravitated towards the dresser. He opened each drawer and judged its contents. "So, are you still going to give us a tour, or should we snoop through your belongings and come to our own conclusions?"

Cobalt marched over to the dresser and firmly shut the drawer his nosy brother was looking at. "No," he stated. "Come with me."

Crimson shot a shifty look over his shoulder, then muttered, "I *saw* that polyester blend. You can't hide your sins from me."

Thystle rolled his eyes and dragged Crimson away from the dresser before he set it on fire.

Cobalt stood by the hidden door with his brothers gathered behind him. He was quiet for a few moments. I could tell he was nervous. I wished I could telepathically transfer some of my relaxed energy to him.

"It's okay, Cobalt," I promised. "Nobody's gonna judge your hoard."

Cobalt turned his gaze on his suit-wearing brother. "Even though Crimson *just* insulted my wardrobe?" he countered.

"That's different," Crimson argued. "That heinous shirt isn't part of your hoard." He paused, suddenly looking horrified. "Unless it is, in which case, Holy Drake save your soul."

"It's not," Cobalt said.

Crimson deflated with sheer relief.

"Seriously, Cobalt, we all love you and respect you," Thystle chimed in. "That includes your hoard. We may poke fun at each other sometimes, but we don't really mean it."

Cobalt's expression relaxed around the edges. I knew that hearing his brother say they loved him must've melted his heart a little. Underneath his big strong appearance, he was a huge softie.

"He's right," Jade said with an encouraging smile. "Whatever lurks beyond this door is your passion. We're dragons, Cobalt. We *all* understand that."

Since I wasn't a dragon, I'd never fully know what it felt like to have a hoard, but I knew it was deeply special to each individual. Maybe it was the way I felt about Blueberry, but times a million.

The resolve hardened on Cobalt's face. Having his brothers' unconditional support gave him the last scrap of strength he needed to open the door.

"All right," Cobalt said. "Come inside."

I smiled as the brothers excitedly burst into the aquarium chamber. Its blue light spilled out into the bedroom. It reminded me of the egg's glow.

I rubbed the shell's sides. In the past few days, it exuded more warmth than usual. I was all for the egg taking its time to hatch, but I was keen to see my baby, too.

"Must be tough waiting."

Viol's gruff comment startled me. I whipped around to see him standing by the bed. His sharp purple eyes were focused on the egg.

"Oh, hey, Viol," I greeted.

He looked confused when I patted the space next to me for him to sit down, but sat anyway. He perched on the furthest possible edge, keeping his distance from me, almost like he was afraid to get too close. Maybe he didn't want to accidentally poke my eye out with the studs on his leather jacket. What a thoughtful guy.

"Not interested in Cobalt's hoard?" I asked, nodding at the open chamber. I heard the dragons' voices mingling in excitement as Cobalt gave them a tour.

Viol snorted. "What do I care about another dragon's hoard? Egg's more interesting."

Underneath his hard tone was a current of softness, one he couldn't hide.

I grinned. "Do you wanna touch it?"

His eyes widened. Slowly, he asked, "Can I?"

"'Course you can."

Viol's calloused hand trembled as he reached for the egg. He placed his palm on the shell with great reverence. The intensity of Viol's dark eyes softened as he stroked the eggshell. Then, as if he couldn't bear to touch it a second longer, he drew his hand back and abruptly stood up.

"Thanks," he mumbled roughly.

"No prob."

By the time I got the two words out, he'd already hurried out the door.

I shrugged and glanced down at the egg. "Uncle Viol's a funny guy, isn't—"

The rest of my sentence came out as incomprehensible gibberish.

Because there was a big hole in the egg.

And a tiny blue paw sticking out of it.

"Uh," I said, my voice raising in volume. "Um, um, um?"

Cobalt stuck his head into the bedroom. "Is everything all right, Muzo?"

I flubbed my words until I finally blurted out, "*Egg.*"

Cobalt couldn't see the hole from his angle. He furrowed his brow in confusion. "Yes, that's right. We have an egg together."

I grabbed the discarded piece of shell and waved it in the air frantically to get my message across.

Cobalt's eyes widened with understanding. He rushed over to the bed, then gasped when he saw the hole.

"The egg," he uttered.

"That's what I'm saying!" I cried.

Cobalt's breathing quickened as he leaned in to watch the dragonet's tiny paw move around. I was shocked at the newborn's mobility—hell, it wasn't even technically *born* yet, since most of its body was still trapped inside the shell.

"C'mon, you can do it," I urged.

"What's going on out here?" Saffron asked, nosily sticking his head into the bedroom. When he saw me and Cobalt hovering next to the egg, he yelped and ran over. "Is the egg hatching? Oh Holy Drake, it's hatching. Everyone, get your asses in here!"

The urgency in Saffron's voice summoned all the dragons from the other room. Crimson and Thystle—the seasoned parents—gave us room to breathe, along with Jade, who naturally figured we needed space. On the other hand, Aurum and Saffron were all up in the egg's business, unable to contain their curiosity. Saffron's golden eyes beamed with interest, while Aurum's gleamed with guarded wonder.

Cobalt squeezed my hand. "Look."

Apparently, our egg appreciated an audience. It threw itself onto the quilt and rolled in a circle. A flurry of annoyed squeaks echoed inside the shell.

"Good, healthy pair of lungs," Cobalt commented warmly. The baby hadn't fully hatched yet and he already radiated with pride.

The dragonet kicked hard. A piece of shell flew off the egg and hit Aurum in the face.

"Ow!"

"Haha," Saffron said a moment before another chunk of eggshell smacked him, too. "Ow!"

Aurum rubbed his cheek. "Damn, not even born and already attacking their uncles..."

I snorted with laughter. Our baby had a feisty attitude all right. It made me even more excited for the last pieces of the eggshell to fall.

My heart squeezed like I was on a roller coaster. Cobalt's shoulder brushed against mine, a calming reminder of his presence. This moment we shared was magical, and I was so happy to be here with him.

Finally, the top half of the shell cracked open, and a little blue dragonet exploded upwards with a triumphant baby roar.

The floodgates to my parental instincts burst. Tears of joy sprung to my eyes. Suddenly overwhelmed with emotion, I picked up my baby. The little blue dragon whimpered and squirmed, but calmed down once pressed to my chest. A warm, dreamy feeling spread throughout my body. It was a kind of happiness I'd never experienced before—similar to my love for Cobalt, but different. It was deep and ancient and protective.

The instinctual overload tipped me into shifting. Once I was in jackal form, I licked my baby dragonet from head to tail. They protested with an irritable squeak.

Once my jackal soul was satisfied, I shifted back with a sigh. "There we go. All clean."

Cobalt chuckled and reached for the baby. "Good job, Daddy Muzo."

I grinned. "Daddy Muzo, huh? I like the sound of that. What are we gonna call *you*, Cobalt?"

He smiled as he gazed into the baby's eyes. "I want to be Papa."

"Aww," Saffron cooed.

Aurum snorted. "Okay, even I have to admit, that's kinda cute."

A dark figure skidded in the doorway, then rushed inside. Viol breathed hard, like he'd run all the way back here.

"Is the baby——" He stopped, eyes widening when he saw the dragonet. "Oh."

Every hard line and sharp edge of his face softened. He stepped closer, standing in line with the rest of his brothers as he gazed upon the baby.

"They're beautiful," Viol murmured.

I could barely hear him. It was almost like he was talking to himself.

"What's this cutie's name? Do you have one yet? Ooh, if you don't, can I pick one?" Saffron begged.

Aurum snorted. "Nobody wants the crappy names you cooked up, bro."

"Shut up, they're not crappy!"

"Nobody can spell Phthalo, let alone say it."

"But it's cool, and it means blue!"

Cobalt raised a hand to cool the twins' argument. "Thanks, you two, but we already picked a name. You know, as a couple?" he added, raising a brow.

Crimson stepped in to grab the twins by the backs of their shirts. "Yes, and now the couple gets to enjoy alone time with their newborn without Thing 1 and Thing 2 bothering them."

"Hey, I don't consent to being thrown out!" Aurum pleaded as Crimson dragged him outside.

Saffron was also being hauled out of the room as he cried, "Yeah, we don't even know the baby's name yet!"

Cobalt and I exchanged an amused look. I decided to break their suspense.

"It's Lazuli!" I called.

"Oh shit, that's an awesome name!" Saffron's ecstatic voice called back from around the corner.

"Thanks!"

After congratulating us and wishing us the best, the rest of Cobalt's brothers followed suit until the bedroom contained only our little family of three.

Four, if you counted Blueberry.

TWENTY-SIX

Cobalt

LAZULI BLINKED at the aquarium with electric-blue eyes. Their sky-blue scales seemed to glow beside the dappled light of the tank. In the weeks since they'd hatched from their egg, their rambunctious, loud personality shone through every second. I couldn't remember what I was like as a young dragonet, but I wasn't as boisterous as Lazuli.

Yet whenever we plopped Lazuli in front of my hoard, their demeanor changed. They went silent as a mouse, content to stare at the dancing kelp, darting fish, and slow-moving river snails.

"Isn't it weird?" Muzo asked. "I mean, no offense to you or your hoard, obviously—but for a kid, you'd think it'd be boring to watch." He nodded at Lazuli sitting comfortably on a pillow, their snout inches from the glass. "But our kid's obsessed."

"I'm not offended," I assured him. "I'm aware that it's boring to most people."

"Except me," Muzo pointed out.

"Except you."

Muzo kneeled down and patted our dragonet's head.

"And Lazuli. Maybe they're gonna grow up to hoard snails too, eh, Cobalt?"

I chuckled at the idea. "I highly doubt that. Dragon hoard affinities aren't genetic, as you can tell from my brothers."

"How was your little tour, by the way?" Muzo asked, tilting his head.

"It was nice," I said, glancing up at the tank. I watched the resident pair of snails share a fresh cucumber slice. "They asked me questions. A lot of them. It was like... they really cared. I didn't expect that." I smiled at my mate. "You were right after all."

Muzo's grin lit up his face. "See? I told you! Man, I wish I could've seen it. I wanted to eavesdrop, but as soon as you guys left the bedroom, Viol showed up to chat."

My brows rose. "He did?"

Muzo sat next to Lazuli on the pillow. "Yup. He was super interested in Lazuli's egg."

I recalled all the times Viol offered to babysit Ruby, Heather, and now Lazuli, too. His keen affection for his young charges was only matched by his hostility toward us. But he wasn't nasty to Taylor, Matteo, or Muzo. In fact, the three omegas had a completely different relationship with him than we dragons did. I wondered if he cleaned up his attitude for them since they were newcomers to our family, or if he just had a soft spot for omegas and children.

But then I remembered our confrontation before the Dragonfate Games began. Viol's aggressive concern for my safety stopped me from leaving the island to chase Muzo down. It wasn't jealousy, or that he wanted to keep us apart. Viol *wanted* me to find my fated mate, but deep down, he was fueled by fear.

I found that odd. Viol was harsh, rough, and cold. Why should a man like him be afraid of anything?

My protective instincts had evolved since falling in love with Muzo, and Lazuli's hatching. They were stronger than ever, and they extended to my entire family. Whatever was paining my brother, I wanted to know.

"I'm going to talk to Viol," I said, scooping up my dragonet.

"And you're bringing Lazuli as a bribe?"

"Exactly."

Muzo chuckled. "Have fun. I'll stay here and keep feeding the snails."

"Not too many treats, remember?"

"I know, I know." He reached into the food bucket and pulled out an apple slice. "I'll keep it to one. Or three. Or seven."

I huffed in amusement at his antics. I'd never win this battle, but that was fine. An extra apple slice or two or seven never hurt anybody. Besides, the shrimp and fish did an excellent job polishing off the extraneous treats Muzo snuck into the tank when he thought I wasn't looking.

On my way out of the bedroom, I noticed something off. I squinted at the bed.

Blueberry was gone again.

I sighed. This was a regular occurrence lately. Blueberry would go missing, then conveniently show up, then disappear once more. It was like the thing had a mind of its own. Either that, or there was a plushie-kidnapping crusader in our midst.

I thanked Holy Drake that Lazuli didn't give a damn about the plush toy, otherwise I'd put more effort into getting him back. But unlike his baby, Muzo *did* care about Blueberry. He went frantic every time the plushie went missing. I considered commissioning Taylor for an identical one so Blueberry Version 1.0 could live his life in peace, wherever he was.

"Ready to see Uncle Viol?" I asked Lazuli on the way to his room.

Lazuli let out a tiny, eager growl.

They couldn't speak yet, and hadn't yet had their first shift, but that was normal for a dragonet their age. I enjoyed this sweet age to the fullest, and I couldn't wait to see the person they'd become.

Viol answered on the first knock. "What?" he snapped before his gaze fell on Lazuli in my arms. "Oh. Hi, sweetie."

"I wasn't aware we were that close," I joked.

He arched a brow. "Using your kid as an emotional shield is dark-sided, Cobalt." His cold expression broke into a smirk. "I like that."

"Speaking of emotional shields, let's talk... Violet."

Viol's dark eyes flashed. He bristled like a jungle cat about to spring, but when I plopped Lazuli in his arms, all his bluster fell away. His face warred with itself. Eventually it settled into a half smile, half snarl as he snuggled a very happy Lazuli close to his chest.

"What do you want?" Viol growled at me.

I didn't bother wasting time. I'd already skipped straight to conflict by addressing Viol by his full name. There was no use beating around the bush now.

"What happened to you?" I asked quietly.

He side-eyed me. "Gonna have to be specific."

"You know exactly what I mean," I said, matching his unyielding tone. "As a teenager, when you left the island. What happened? What changed you?"

Viol stared at me for a few long moments before yanking his gaze away and glowering in the opposite direction. "Why do you care?"

"Because you're my brother, and I love you," I said.

He groaned. "Gross. You've been an overemotional sap since you became a dad."

I decided not to bring up the fact that if anyone was uncharacteristically emotional about the concept of parenthood and children, it was him.

"It's not gross, and I don't care if you think that," I stated. "It's the truth. You're different than you were back then. I just want to know why."

His face hardened. "It won't change anything. So, why don't you focus on me *now*?"

I blinked. That statement rewired the way I thought about the situation. He had a point. Sating my curiosity wouldn't help Viol with whatever inner turmoil he faced— but supporting him in the present moment would.

"You're right. I'm sorry," I said.

Viol stopped scowling. Just as his words perplexed me, mine had the same effect on him.

"No matter what happened, just know that I care, and that I'm here for you. We all are," I promised. I gently took Lazuli's paw and patted Viol's chest with it. "Even Lazuli."

The last of Viol's guard crumbled. He breathed out a rough laugh. "Especially Lazuli."

I remembered Muzo back at my hoard chamber. I itched to return to his side. He'd made it abundantly clear that he wanted some *special* alone time.

"Do you feel like babysitting this afternoon?" I asked Viol.

Viol hiked Lazuli up in his arms with a grin. "Do I? What d'you think, Laz? Should we have a play date with Ruby and Heather?"

Lazuli playfully chomped his finger, which in dragonet terms was a resounding yes.

I RETURNED to my hoard to find Muzo bouncing off the walls like a kid overdosed on sugar.

"I didn't realize you were *that* excited for alone time," I teased.

Muzo slammed into me, pointing frantically at the tank. "Cobalt, Cobalt, Cobalt—"

I was starting to think his explosive excitement wasn't about sex. "What is it?" I asked, following his gesture. Aside from the seven illicit apple slices, I didn't see anything out of the ordinary. The tank looked the same as ever.

"The snails!" Muzo cried. "They did it!"

"Did what?"

Muzo grunted in exasperation. "Oh, just *come* and *see*!" He ran behind me and shoved me closer to the aquarium, then jabbed his finger against the glass. "There!"

I focused on where Muzo was pointing—and then I saw it.

The baby river snail.

There were *three* Chromatimaeus river snails in the tank.

"They did it," I breathed, shocked and elated to my core. "They actually did it."

Muzo shook my arm, unable to control his excitement. "I told you! They literally did it! I don't know *how*, 'cause I don't know anything about snail sex, but that's okay because they had a baby together!"

His giddiness infected me. I chuckled and hugged him as he bounced up and down. His zest for life always uplifted me. I couldn't remember what my life had been like before him, and I didn't want to. The only thing that mattered was our bright future.

"We gotta name the baby snail," Muzo announced.

"Sure. But the parents don't even have names," I reminded him.

He pointed at the big snails. "Okay, how about this. That one's Apple, and that one's Cucumber."

"I see you're a fan of food-themed names."

"Oh, just wait until you hear the name I had in mind for the baby." Muzo grinned. "How about... Raspberry? 'Cause it's small and cute like a raspberry?"

I pressed a kiss to his cheek. "Raspberry is perfect. And it matches with Blueberry."

I wondered if I should tell him about Blueberry's latest disappearance, worried it might distract from his happiness, but Muzo was currently too enthralled by the infant mollusc to worry about his adventuring plushie. It was sweet how his parental instincts extended to the smallest of creatures.

Emotion swelled within me and I hugged Muzo tighter. Of course my fated mate cared about baby snails—they were part of my hoard, after all. We were truly destined to be together.

In the shimmering blue light of the aquarium, Muzo took my breath away. The ever-present joy in his eyes was a gift that soothed my soul. Yet he was more than the happy-go-lucky clown most people saw. He was kind, compassionate, and strong. We saw the truth in each other, and that was more than I could ever ask for.

"I love you," I murmured in his ear.

He lifted his head to beam at me. "Love you most-est."

"Love you most-est-er."

He laughed. "Okay, that one is *so* not a word."

"Let's make it one. I'll have Jade add it to the official dictionary."

Muzo tilted his head curiously. "Is that a real thing he can do?"

I smiled. "Why don't we go and find out?"

Muzo grabbed my hand, eager for any adventure we embarked on together.

TWENTY-SEVEN

Epilogue: Muzo

"UH, MUZO? WHAT ARE YOU DOING?"

Aurum's question made my ears flick in his direction. I had all four paws and my nose to the floor. Beside me, Lazuli did the same. My kid was excellent at copying me—especially when it involved getting into mischief.

But this was no mischief. This was very important work.

"I'm teaching Lazuli how to track scents," I clarified. "It's part of their jackal heritage."

"Okay," Aurum said, still confused. "And why exactly are you doing it outside our bedroom?"

"It just happened to be on my route. The scent trail leads around here *somewhere*, I know it..."

Saffron either heard the commotion, or was psychically summoned by his twin, or both. He stuck his head out the door, then gasped. "Lazuli! Hi!"

He reached to pick Lazuli up, but the dragonet chomped Saffron's hand. Clearly, snuffling around on the floor was more fun than being held in their uncle's arms.

"Ow," Saffron mumbled, nursing a baby bite wound.

Aurum snorted. "Serves you right. Not every infant wants to be captured and doted on by you."

"Well, they should," Saffron argued. "Wait, so what's going on again?"

"Muzo and Lazuli are tracking a scent," Aurum explained.

"Oh. Why?"

"Because Blueberry's missing for the three-millionth time," I said.

Saffron gasped in horror. "No!"

"What are *you* so upset about?" Aurum asked.

"Because I also asked Taylor to sew me a plush dragon," Saffron uttered, his face pale. "What if the thief steals that, too?"

Aurum pulled a face. "Guys, come on. They're toys, not priceless artifacts."

Taylor's dry voice interjected. "Say that again after I spent hours patterning and hand sewing those one-of-a-kind *toys*."

He silently appeared out of nowhere with his usual tiger's grace.

Now Aurum was the one going pale. He began to stammer. "Sorry, Taylor, I didn't mean—"

But he didn't get far. Saffron and I instantly noticed that Taylor hadn't joined our conversation empty-handed. He carried not one but two dragon plushies—one blue, and one yellow.

"PLUSHIES!" we yelled simultaneously.

Taylor chuckled at our zeal. He tossed me the blue one and handed the yellow one to Saffron. The yellow-haired twin lit up like a neon sign, squeezing the matching dragon to his chest. "Look at him! He looks just like me. I think I'll call him Saffron Jr."

"The resemblance is uncanny," Aurum remarked.

Meanwhile, I was thrilled to have my plushie back. "Taylor! You found Blueberry!"

"Not quite," Taylor said, nodding behind me.

I turned around to see Cobalt kneeling there. My tail wagged instinctively.

My alpha smiled. "Blueberry kept going missing, so I asked Taylor to make a second one. Hopefully Blueberry 2.0 will stay put."

My mate was always thinking about me. My tail wagged harder, thumping against the floor. "Cobalt! You're amazing."

"Anything for you," he said, petting my head.

Lazuli tilted their head, then reached for Blueberry 2.0 with their dragon paws. I exchanged a surprised glance with Cobalt. Our baby had never expressed interest in the toy before.

"You want him?" I asked, then placed him on the floor in front of Lazuli. "Here."

Lazuli looked the toy up and down, which was adorable since they were the same size. Then they flopped forward into a hug.

Not even Aurum could withstand the explosion of cuteness. His face melted and he echoed his twin's loud "Aww."

I saw the purest vision of fatherly love on Cobalt's face. It wasn't the first time I'd see that expression, and it wouldn't be the last, but each and every time, it made me a thousand times more attracted to him—if that was even possible.

"Hey, Saffron," I said.

He paused hugging his new plushie for a second. "Yeah?"

"You feel like babysitting tonight?"

He immediately shoved Saffron Jr into Aurum's hands.

"Yes! Finally!"

"What am I supposed to do with this thing?" his twin grumbled.

Saffron ignored him. Instead of scooping up Lazuli like he'd tried earlier, he lay on the floor beside them. "We're gonna have an awesome time. Right, Zuzu?"

Lazuli squeaked happily. They didn't bite their uncle this time.

AS COBALT WHISKED me away to our bedroom, I couldn't help but wonder what happened to Blueberry 1.0.

"Do you think he's okay, wherever he is?" I asked.

"I'm sure he's just fine." He kissed the corner of my mouth, then teased, "Aren't you supposed to be the optimistic one?"

"True. I guess if *you* think he's okay, then he must be."

Cobalt laid me on top of the bed, his massive frame looming deliciously over me.

"Why don't I take your mind off it?" he suggested in a draconic purr.

My blood shivered with hot anticipation. "Mm, don't mind if you do..."

THE END

Will Aurum's stubbornness never to fall in love last when he finds his fated mate? Find out in Alpha Dragon's Ferret!

Want to witness the cereal incident that causes Lazuli's first shift? Grab the exclusive bonus scene by signing up to my newsletter!

Also by Hawke Oakley

The Dragonfate Games

Possessive and loving alpha dragons find their fated mates on a reality TV show set on a private beach!

Awakened Womb

Human men crash land on an alien planet, and unexpectedly find love—and pregnancies.

Fairytale Mates Series

Fluffy, sweet fated mates novellas! Each book features a mythical shifter alpha and his human omega.

Pack of Heirs Series

The sequel to Pack of Brothers, these shifter books are filled with heat, magic and intrigue!

Pack of Brothers Series

A fated mates series featuring mismatched shifter pairings, often predator and prey!

Cursed Alphas Series

Gothic-flavor monster romance!

Alpha Market Series

A dark series where omegas rule over alphas, featuring a twist on the concept of fated mates!

Dragons of Cinderhollow Series

Omega For All Series

Omega Angel Café Series

Tenebrae Brothers Series

Indigo Mountain Pack Series

Laced Fates Series

Whitewood Pack Duology

MM Shifter Romance

Grizzly Heat

MM Contemporary Romance

Love Me, Hate Me

Heart of Light

Mistletoe Madness

**MM Contemporary Romance Novels
(Written as Anders Grey)**

Blooming Desire Series

Stray Hearts Series

Breaking the Ice

Printed in Great Britain
by Amazon